THE ILLUSION OF A BOY

LeeAnn Werner

To those who seek.

"In the universe, there are things that are known, and things that are unknown, and in between, there are doors."

—WILLIAM BLAKE, POET

ACKNOWLEDGEMENTS

Thank you to my husband Wulf, my biggest fan and constant source of support.

CONTENTS

CHAPTER 1

JESSIE

A fiery spark rocketed upward from the earth and burned through the dark sky. As gravity pulled it toward the ground, it shimmered into the golden shape of a palm tree. My lips flicked upward into a smile at the sight of my favorite firework. I walked Baby, our little black mutt, toward the large, grassy hill in the middle of Hunter Park.

Night was my preferred time to walk, as it hid my identity. In our neighborhood, suspicions and questions about his death surrounded me like a shroud. But Baby provided a good cover. I was a nameless girl with her dog.

I'd wanted to do a lot of things in silence since my dad died. It took too much energy to talk, to force my thoughts into words. It wasn't worth the effort.

Grandma tried to hide her hurt feelings when I didn't invite her on a walk. Tonight, it hadn't been necessary, as she was spending the weekend with friends.

I shook my head, trying to dislodge the thoughts of his death—and the questions I still had. He died in the woods, but I had no idea how he ended up there or why he'd died. Bottom line: I was relieved. His death meant the abuse was finally over.

A striking Fourth of July display exploded overhead as I settled in with Baby. I chose a grassy spot on the outskirts of the crowd.

My fellow firework-watchers chatted and wrangled their children. Cans cracked open, and the aroma of beer hung in the humid summer air. The deep booms of the fireworks resonated through my body. Orbs of gold, blue, and red flashed across the night sky and then crackled back to the ground. Baby pressed herself against me and trembled. I squeezed her to my chest.

"You're fine. You're fine," I whispered into her black, silky ear.

I should have left her at home, but I had been too uncomfortable to watch the fireworks completely alone.

Mom had been staring blankly at the TV when I left. Severe depression had plagued her since my father's death. Inconceivably, she missed him. She thought they had been in love. Her continued delusion angered me and drove me crazy. Of course, he had been *slightly* less abusive to her.

She hadn't even turned her head to acknowledge my goodbye. Instead of our lives getting instantly easier with his death, they transitioned to providing constant care. Pushing down my feelings of frustration, I smirked. On the bright side, I wasn't afraid for my life anymore.

Grandma had been keeping Mom under close watch, but she needed a break. We all did. I didn't mind Grandma taking some time for herself. She had taken on most of the care.

Four months had dragged on while we processed the shock of Dad's absence. Like the walking wounded, Brian, my brother, and I were so grateful the nightmare was finally over but were still dealing with the carnage.

Mom barely got out of bed unless Grandma made her eat or shower. I assured myself she would be OK watching TV for a bit. Crinkling my brow, I wondered whether her doctor was giving her too much medication.

The mosquitos buzzed incessantly around my long, dark hair. I swatted at the light tickles on my legs. A slight breeze brought a little relief, but not much. Sweat trickled down my back and beneath the waistband of my shorts. After thirty minutes of the swirling death match, I gave up battling the mosquitos and walked back toward my house, brushing the grass from the back of my shorts.

"Jessie?"

I jumped and wheeled around to find Will, my classmate, previous kissing partner, and the blond Adonis of my dreams.

"Oh hey, how are you?" I said. My mouth had become a desert wasteland.

His profile was like a Greek statue, with its strong jaw and nose. It wasn't just his looks that attracted me. He cared about me. He had shown up to support me over and over again, such as after my car accident and, most importantly, during my dad's search party.

There were moments I couldn't remember about that day. My cheeks flamed with embarrassment. Will's warm and caring embrace before the hunt for my dad was the only thing I did recall.

"Better now. I'm glad I spotted you," he said. Even in the darkness, his eyes eagerly searched my face.

My heart pounded as he began to walk beside me. "Are you here with friends?"

"Yeah." He nodded toward them with a smile. "But they can live without me for a few minutes."

I hadn't seen Will since the day we found my father dead in the woods.

We had texted a few times, but it had been pretty general. It had been a lonely summer so far. Alex, my cheating ex-boyfriend, was out of the picture. Will had been one bright spot of love and attention.

I didn't blame him for not staying in touch. What do you say to a girl whose parent just died? "I know your dad died recently, but let's go out" wasn't Will's style.

We continued to talk as I made my way back to the house. It was so nice to see him and hear his voice. As it always had, our conversation flowed easily as we ambled along the sidewalk under the canopy of trees. I basked in his attentiveness.

Far too soon, we were back at my house. Will lingered on my front porch, his weight shifting from one leg to the other. He stilled, leaning down to wrap his long, strong arms around me. My face pressed into his chest, and his heart thudded steadily in my ear. My whole body relaxed.

He straightened but kept his hands on my shoulders. "It's good to see you."

My brown eyes locked with his light-blue ones. His hug had soothed my starving soul, and I desperately wanted more.

"It's good to see you too," I said.

Will's face split into a wide smile, revealing perfectly white teeth that screamed, "I wore braces for years." His hands slid down my arms and squeezed my fingers.

"Let's hang out soon. Message me," he said.

"Yeah, I'd like that," I said. Will bent down and patted Baby's head. He smiled and gave me a small wave as he slowly backed away. He couldn't possibly be any cuter.

Humming to myself, I opened my front door and crouched down to let Baby off her leash. I straightened as the door clicked shut behind me.

The house was silent. Every light had been turned off, including the TV. I groped my way toward the kitchen and flipped on the light. A scrap of paper lay on the spotless kitchen counter. I recognized my mom's handwriting.

Don't do drugs. They ruin your life.
Love Mom

My brows furrowed in bewilderment. What in the hell was that supposed to mean? I crumpled the ridiculous piece of paper in my hand. It took only a few seconds to understand.

"No! Mom!" I shrieked, the sound ricocheting through the house. The windows were open, but I didn't care what the neighbors might think of my screams. I thundered toward the hall.

I pushed open her door and flipped on the light. She lay on her bed, curled to the side in the gray sweatshirt and pants she'd had on when I left the house. My whole body trembled as I shook her shoulder. Her mouth dropped open, but she didn't respond.

Footsteps pounded down the hallway. "Jessie?" Will shouted. He ran into her room with wide eyes.

"She tried to kill herself!" I cried while ineffectually gesturing toward her.

Will dug his phone out of his pocket and dialed 911. I stared blankly as he gave the operator the details.

"Is she breathing?" Will asked.

His question made me focus. I watched her chest slightly rise and fall. "Yes."

What had she taken? Her nightstand was empty, so I turned to the adjoining bathroom. A prescription pill bottle lay at the bottom of the white sink with just a few capsules remaining. My hand trembled as I reached for the bottle to quickly scan the label. I wasn't familiar with the medication.

I stood by the bed, rocking back and forth as I watched the minutes tick by. I focused on the shallow rise and fall of her chest. Why had she done this? Didn't Brian and I mean anything to her? Life wasn't worth living if her drunk, abusive husband wasn't around? Rage built within me.

The squawk of the ambulance startled me from my stupor. Will let the EMTs in and led them to the bedroom.

"Miss, do you know what happened?" the paramedic asked.

"She tried to kill herself," I said. Wasn't it obvious? The thought played on a loop in my mind.

My hand trembled as I handed him the pill bottle and the scrap of paper. The paramedic inspected the prescription bottle and read the note with an impassive face. He stuffed them both into his pocket without making eye contact.

Her one-sentence suicide note perfectly demonstrated her delusional mental state. She hadn't said she was sorry for enabling our abuser. She hadn't said she loved us. We didn't do drugs. All of it was utter nonsense. My entire body continued to shake. Why was she like this? Why was she an utter mess? They were my biggest questions.

Will put his arm around my shoulders and held me securely against him. We watched as the paramedics loaded her onto the gurney.

"How did you know to come back?" I said, looking up at him.

"I heard you scream as I was walking down your driveway," he said.

I nodded and mumbled a thank-you. Our eyes met, and in that moment, understanding, sadness, and disbelief passed between us. I didn't know what I would have done without him here. It was a struggle to remain standing, but his comforting presence made the situation somewhat bearable. With Will's support, I was able to function.

I patted my pockets for my phone. I needed to call Brian and get him home.

My brother picked up after a few rings. "Where are you?" I asked.

"Why? What's wrong?" He'd clearly noticed the panicked tone of my voice.

"I need you to meet me at Stanton Hospital. Mom tried to kill herself with pills." Blunt was my mode of operation when freaked out.

"Are you fucking kidding me?" Brian said, all anger. In an instant, worry bled through the phone. "Is she okay?"

"I think so. She's still breathing."

The EMTs carried Mom to the waiting ambulance. Before shutting the doors, the paramedic met my gaze. "Miss, do you want to ride with us to the hospital?"

I looked at Will, who was still standing right beside me.

"I'll take you," he said before I could ask. Thank God. I was clinging to him like a lifeline.

I took a deep breath and shook my head. "I'll just meet you at the emergency room. Will is giving me a ride."

The red lights pulsed into the darkness as they loaded her into the ambulance. The paramedic turned to me. "Be sure you bring your mom's ID," he said.

"I'll get her purse." I ran back into the house and grabbed her handbag from the counter. I would probably need her insurance information too. It was too surreal. How could this be happening? The doors of the ambulance closed as I hustled to Will's car with Mom's purse clutched to my chest.

We followed the ambulance and pulled into the emergency room parking lot. The artificial brightness of the hospital lit the surrounding fir trees and landscaped flower beds.

Will and I stood in the waiting area outside the emergency room, our gazes trained on the door in case Brian showed up. The shock had started to wear off, and anger built in its place.

Of course, she would do this. God forbid we just lived peacefully after Dad's death. Oh no. I lost the biggest stressor of my life, and my mom responded by breaking down completely. I had been gifted the worst parents of all time. Why these two idiots had Brian and me, I had no idea. They clearly couldn't handle themselves, let alone children.

Brian ran into the waiting room, panic stamped across his face. Tracey, his girlfriend, followed just a few steps behind. She rushed over to hug me and then stopped, her arms hanging in the air a moment before they dropped to her sides. Her brows knitted together as she studied my face. She retreated a few steps away. I crossed my arms tightly over my chest, hurt by her odd actions but unwilling to show it. I quickly brought Brian up to speed on Mom's condition, or at least what I understood.

"Hey, Will. Thanks for driving her," Brian said.
"Yeah, no problem. We walked to your house after the fireworks, and that's when we found her," Will said.

Brian nodded and rubbed his fist against the palm of his left hand, a telltale sign he was excited or nervous. He'd done it since we were little.

A middle-aged doctor in light-blue scrubs walked into the waiting area. He scanned the waiting room, his eyes landing on our group. "Miss Taylor?"

I nodded. "Yes."

He exhaled forcefully and came over to us. "And this is?"

"My brother," I answered.

"I'm Dr. Adams. Your mom is in stable condition. We pumped her stomach, but she's resting comfortably now. I don't think she will have any long-term effects from the pills she took, but we'll need to keep her on a psychiatric hold."

"Is she awake? Brian was shocked and confused, but I radiated anger.

"She's very groggy. I would guess she'll sleep for several hours." He cleared his throat. "Is there an adult or any other family with you?" His tanned face wrinkled with concern.

"I'm eighteen, but I will contact our grandmother," Brian answered. "OK, good. Was there an issue that may have led her to this?" the doctor asked.

"Our dad passed away in March," Brian answered.

The doctor's face creased with worry. "I'm sorry for your loss." He paused a moment. "And your current struggle." He squeezed Brian's shoulder.

"Go home and try to get some sleep. They won't let you see her until after nine tomorrow morning," he said.

Relief flooded by body. Hanging out in the hospital for a few more hours would have stoked my anger. I was already furious and frustrated and confused. Why would she do this? I wanted to scream "why" so loudly it would reach the heavens.

Will walked with us to Brian's car. "Call me anytime for whatever you need," he said. Our eyes met, and Will hesitated a moment. Did he feel my anger? He pressed his lips into a grim line and then walked away.

Rage erected an invisible wall around me. Even Will's kind and supportive attention couldn't get through.

CHAPTER 2

BRIAN

The next morning, I kept my thoughts to myself as I drove back to the hospital. Jesus, what a screwed-up mess. Jessie left Mom for thirty minutes to watch fireworks, and Mom tried to kill herself. Mom had seemed slightly more stable lately. She ate more, talked more. Maybe she had been biding her time. I couldn't wrap my head around it.

My hands squeezed the wheel. I had to call Grandma this morning and tell her what had happened. I didn't know how much strain she could take. I was afraid she would have a heart attack when I told her.

Good thing she was a tough old bird. How my mom came from such a strong woman, I had no idea. My mom, needy and weak, was nothing like her mother. The constant need to watch over her drove me nuts. Sometimes I wanted to peel off the responsibility and toss it in the trash like an old Band-Aid. Selfishly, I would be very happy to have Grandma take over once again.

I pushed my slightly long dirty blond hair off my forehead and sighed. *Here we go. Round two of the shit show*, I thought as I pulled into the hospital parking lot. Jessie, who'd been silent for the entire ride, worried me. I glanced over at her. The deep V etched into her brow didn't bode well. I hoped she could keep it together. We both knew her anger could cause unfortunate changes in her personality.

"You ready?" I wiped my palms against my jeans.

"Oh yeah, I love this. Can't get enough," Jessie said.

Anger rolled off my sister. I swallowed hard.

"I need you to remain calm. We don't need additional incidents. Right?"

"Yes, I'll be fine." She huffed, pushed open the car door, and got out, preventing any further conversation.

I took a deep breath. There was nothing else I could do to control Jessie. She knew the risks as well as I did. *Impending doom, here we come.*

I had to jog to catch up to Jessie. She stood by my side as I asked the receptionist where we could find Mom. The woman checked her computer and then pulled out a pouch containing small plastic cards.

"You'll need to wear these to confirm your authorization for our wellness center," the receptionist said as she handed the badges to me. "Just follow the yellow arrows down the hall. They will indicate which way to turn."

I clipped the badge onto my shirt and nodded to her. "Thank you."

"Follow the yellow brick road," Jessie said in a weird, chirpy voice that sent shivers down my spine.

I shook my head and nudged her forward. We made our way to a separate wing of the hospital. My nose burned from the odor of ammonia mixed with illness. The entrance to the wellness center was locked, an intercom system our only access. I pressed the button and waited.

"Yes?" a female voiced asked politely.

"This is Brian and Jessie Taylor. We're here to see our mom, Jan Taylor."

A buzz sounded, and the door swung open. "Please come to the welcome desk."

We walked into an open space brightened by large skylights. Potted plants and greenery were everywhere. An older lady with gray hair tucked into a bun waved us over to the main desk. She smiled with her lips pressed together.

"Hi, could I see your badges please?" She extended her hand.

Jessie and I both handed them over.

She glanced at them. "Thank you." Her eyes took us in briefly. "Your mom is in Room 505, which is just down this hall to your left. She's with her doctor right now though."

"Can we go in? I would like to talk to her doctor," I said.

"Sure, just knock on the door and let them know," she said.

I strode toward her room, and Jessie followed me silently. I knocked on the door, and a bald, older man with glasses opened it a moment later.

"Can I help you?" he asked.

"Yeah, I'm Brian Taylor, and this is my sister, Jessie. You're my mom's doctor?" My voice cracked. I wished Grandma were here. I didn't know how to handle this.

His shoulders relaxed when he heard our names. He stuck out his hand to shake mine.

"I'm Dr. Lewis, your mom's psychiatrist." His eyes reflected pity. He shut Mom's door and stepped into the hallway. His gaze moved from me to Jessie as he slowly shook his head. "You survived."

I frowned. What an odd thing to say. I tilted my head to the side. "I'm sorry, I didn't catch that."

"I said you survived. I understand how difficult it's been for both of you regarding your mom and dad," he said.

This was the psychiatrist Mom had been seeing for the last two years. Based on how badly she had failed us, I wasn't impressed.

A palpable electricity built around Jessie. My right eye twitched nervously. She darted around me and stepped in front of the doctor.

"Why didn't you help us? Aren't you supposed to report child abuse?" Hands firmly on her hips, she hissed at him.

The doctor's eyes widened.

"Did you do anything to help her? You know, like maybe advise her to leave her drunk husband!" Jessie spat the words in his face. Toe tapping, she waited for her statement to sink in. "Maybe, I don't know, you could have prompted her to not let our dad beat us!"

Were people watching us? Scanning the room, I spotted several wide eyes staring at my sister.

This wasn't Jessie anymore. Lena, my sister's alternate personality, had taken over. An adult noticing Jessie's violent alter was my biggest fear. I worried the cops would reopen Dad's case and take a closer look at my sister's actions the night of his death.

"Do you believe this?" Lena stared at me in disbelief. She turned back to the doctor and screamed, "You did nothing!"

With a white-knuckled grip on his shoulders, she pushed him against the wall. The doctor was at least a foot taller than her, yet she handled him like he weighed nothing.

My paralysis broke. "Stop!" I grabbed Lena's shoulders and tried to pull her away. Electricity shot through my hands and ran up my arms. My jaw clenched and locked. The doctor yelled for security.

"I'm not done with him," she said, clearly enunciating every word. "I'm going to insist you help our mom get her head straight. Figure out the right meds or something, and do it quickly. Because if you don't, I'm going to add you to my list, just like dear old Dad."

God help us. She just mentioned threatening Dad. I tried to pull her back, but she shook me off. One hand clutched the doctor's shirt, while the other moved down his body until she reached his crotch. She gripped his balls and twisted hard.

The doctor gasped and tried to scream for security again, but no sound came from his gaping mouth.

"Consider this your only warning." Lena's voice was full of menace. She released him and stepped away as he slid down the wall. She winked at me and said, "I think he gets it now."

Out of the corner of my eye, I spotted a female security guard running toward us.

"Fantastic! Check this out." Lena motioned to the approaching guard. She beamed at me. "Could this day get any better?"

She charged the security guard, running at full speed. Shit, she was fast. I tackled her just before she reached the guard. The full weight of my body pressed her to the cold linoleum floor. I outweighed my sister by seventy pounds, but it didn't seem like it.

Hanging on to Lena was what I imagined holding on to a tiger would be like. Strength and flexibility radiated from every possible muscle. Her whole body vibrated. My stomach twisted, but I wouldn't let go.

"Lena, stop it. It's Brian. Stop now," I gasped in her ear. She rammed the back of her skull into mine. Pain exploded throughout my head, and white stars popped in my vision.

Semiconscious, I held on. The security guard yelled for me to stop. A herd of nurses, staff, and security pounded toward us. Finally, Lena relaxed underneath me. Jessie's familiar energy returned.

I rolled off and put my hands up.

"We're fine. We're fine. She's fine," I mumbled, still dazed.

I turned toward her and grabbed her shoulder. "Get up," I said. She didn't move. Her mouth hung open, and her eyes rolled up in her head. I gripped both of her shoulders and pulled her to my chest. Her head lolled backward. Panic shot through my body, sending my heart racing. What had Lena's presence done to her? I could not bear losing my sister.

An audience of security and staff surrounded us. A doctor pushed through the gathered crowd and knelt beside us to check Jessie's wrist for a pulse. His hand moved quickly to her neck. He peeled one eyelid back and shined a flashlight in her eye.

He motioned to a nurse. "Get a board. She needs to go to the ER."

CHAPTER 3

JESSIE

I dwelled in the darkness of my dreams. Fear vibrated through me as I slowly walked down the hallway toward Brian's room. My fingers lightly grazed the wall. Some unknown force was pulling me to his room. There was something I had to know.

The house was lit with an odd blue-gray glow. The sun had set, and no one else was home. I stopped at my open bedroom door and peeked in. No, not here. Whatever it was that called me forward, it waited in Brian's room.

Two more steps, and I stood in his doorway. His room had the same shabby blue carpet as mine, a beat-up dresser, and a twin bed. Brian's light-blue comforter covered the bed. I couldn't bring myself to step into the room.

My eyes were drawn to the far corner. A black shape was crouched there. It was a rotation of black dots, hundreds of them swirling clockwise. But it wasn't solid; I could make out the cream wall behind it.

Run!

My gut demanded action, but I was fascinated. I studied the shape. What was it?

My nerves pinged danger to my brain, and my muscles tensed to run. I turned away but managed only a few steps down the hall before the shape hurled itself at me.

A cold, damp force rammed into me. My eyes bulged, and my stomach heaved. My throat was full. I sank to my hands and knees. This thing invaded my body and mind like black sludge. I could feel myself being compressed, pushed down into nothing.

I called for Brian, but the sound was trapped within the black sludge surrounding me. The pressure overwhelmed me. I had to get this off. My mind screamed "GET OUT! GET OUT!"

I pushed against the shape, but my hands met no resistance. It wasn't physical. I had to mentally push it out. I thought about white light, a protective energy, coming from my heart and radiating outward. Where had this idea come from? I didn't know, but I trusted it. I focused on my heart, conjuring a white light, and making it bigger. Slowly, it pushed the darkness out of me.

The shape shrank bit by bit as I pushed my energy to grow larger. Sweat broke out all over my body. Exhausted, I didn't know if I could continue.

I gasped for air, and my body jerked into consciousness. Brian was hunched over me, his face twisted with worry.

"Brian!" I cried. My hands reached for him frantically. "Help me, I can't get it out. I can't breathe." I swiped at my head and face, as if I could wipe the blackness away.

"It's okay, you're okay." Brian got ahold of my hands and held them in his. His brow was deeply furrowed.

"Get it off me!" I screamed.

"There's nothing wrong. Nothing is on you." Brian's expression pleaded for me to believe him. "You're safe, Jessie. You're at the hospital, and you're safe."

Scratchy sheets, white walls, and an antiseptic smell confirmed I was in a hospital room. Dark circles were stamped under Brian's tired blue eyes. He had a large, red, angry bump on his forehead.

"What happened to you?" I asked frowning.

"You headbutted me, and I had to wrestle you to the ground," he said.

"What!? You're crazy." I shook my head. An incessant beeping echoed in the room.

The IV in my arm stung as I pulled against it. Why was I in a hospital gown? "What's happening? Why am I in a hospital bed?"

"Do you remember coming to the hospital to see Mom this morning?" he said slowly and deliberately. Sweat beaded on his forehead.

"No," I said. But my head thudded dully, and I was incredibly tired—just like the other times when I didn't remember something I had done. My scalp prickled in fear.

"You attacked Mom's doctor. They think you're in shock or something. They've sedated you." Brian freed one of his hands to push sweaty hair off his forehead.

The beeping increased.

"Jessie, calm down." Brian squeezed my hand. His eyes flicked to a monitor beside my bed.

"Why am I here?"

"I told you. You attacked Mom's doctor."

I shook my head. I still couldn't believe it had happened. And so publicly. "No. *No.*"

Oh my God. What had I done?

"You threatened him too. You had one of your violent episodes in front of a bunch of hospital staff. I don't know what's going to happen," he said.

Overwhelmed, I felt frantically for my IV line. I needed to get out of here. I needed to run away.

"I want to go home." I said. My fingers found the tape securing the IV to my skin, but I couldn't lift the adhesive. Instead, I yanked at the tubing. The needle stung and burned beneath the thin skin on the top of my hand.

"Stop doing that." Brian jerked my hand away from the IV. "I'll ask the nurse to take it out."

He gathered both of my hands again. "Take a deep breath." His eyes darted to the monitor beside me again.

"What's the beeping noise?" I asked.

"It's your heart. It's beating too fast," he said.

A nurse hurried into the room. Brian stepped away from my bed. The nurse held a syringe.

"No, I don't want any medication." I pushed my hand toward her, palm up. My head swiveled to Brian. "Don't let her sedate me."

Sedation might paralyze me and make me completely helpless against the suffocating black sludge.

"It's OK. You'll be OK." Brian started toward me but hesitated.

The nurse moved forward and quickly injected the contents of the syringe.

Dread overtook me. I wouldn't be able to fight off the black shape. A few seconds passed, and the sedation pulled me back into darkness.

CHAPTER 4

BRIAN

Tears rolled down the side of her face. "I can't fight it off. Help me," she pleaded. Her eyes rolled back in her head, and her eyelids fluttered closed.

Her panic spread to me. I scanned her body. There was nothing wrong that I could see. I took a big breath and wiped the sweat from my face with my sleeve. Pretty soon, they were going to check us all into the hospital. Could someone knock my ass out so I could forget the last twenty-four hours?

"You can wait in the waiting room." The nurse met my gaze kindly. "The doctor wants Jessie to rest."

"My grandmother will be here soon," I said. "She'll want to see her right away."

"For now, the doctor doesn't want any visitors until her heart rate comes down and remains that way."

I eyed the monitor. Even when Jessie was unconscious, her heart pounded away. The screen read 154 beats per minute. It was way too high; my own heart rate would only get that high if I was sprinting.

"Okay," I said. They wouldn't keep my grandmother out of this room, but they could deal with that when she arrived. I rubbed my fist against my palm and wandered to the waiting room. I sank into one of the blue leather chairs.

I wanted to tell—no, needed to tell—Grandma about Jessie's alternate personality, but there was no way I would. Protecting my sister was my priority, and I couldn't risk Grandma asking questions that would put her at risk. I lived in constant fear that Jessie's behavior would in some way be tied to Dad's death. I would take the information Lena shared with me about that night to my grave.

A rush of air and the smell of Grandma's perfume alerted me to her arrival. Her short, silver hair stuck up a little in the back, as if she hadn't taken the time to brush it.

"Brian, what's happened?" Grandma asked as she embraced me.

Her presence comforted me. My shoulders sagged with relief, and I explained what had happened: Mom's suicide attempt. Jessie's attack on the psychiatrist. How Jessie had collapsed, and the way her heart pounded unnaturally fast.

As the words tumbled from my mouth, Grandma's brows rose in disbelief and then furrowed.

"Take me to Jessie, and then I'll go to your mom," she said.

"They don't want anyone in Jessie's room right now," I said.

"I have to see her," Grandma spat, taking my elbow, and propelling me out of the waiting room. I hurried to keep up. The old woman walked faster than I did in her race to Jessie's room.

"Oh, my Lord," Grandma said when she saw Jessie's long, lanky form in the hospital bed. The vital signs monitor beeped away in the background. Grandma hurried to her side and immediately hit the call button.

A female voice answered. "May I help you?"

"Yes, this is Jessica Taylor's grandmother, and I need to speak to her doctor regarding her condition. Immediately."

A young nurse hurried into the room a few minutes later. "Ma'am, the doctor doesn't want visitors…" She faltered at the sight of my grandmother's intense expression.

"I plan to stay with her until the doctor arrives. I'm sure it'll be fine," Grandma said, her lips stretched into a strained smile.

The nurse hesitated but gave a slight nod of her head. "My name is Abby. I'm Jessie's nurse. I'll page the doctor again."

"Thank you," Grandma said, smoothing Jessie's hair back from her face.

I stood there awkwardly. Exhaustion was washing over me now that an adult was here to take the reins.

"Have you seen your mom yet?" Grandma asked.

"No, we were on our way to her room when this all went down," I said.

Grandma sighed. "I'm so mad at her right now. How much more can you kids take?"

She searched my eyes as if I had an answer. I rubbed my face. I had no idea how much more we could handle. The only thing I did know was that I was tired. Tired of the drama. Tired of all this bullshit.

A slightly heavyset doctor in blue scrubs entered our room. "Hello, I'm Dr. Stack, and I'm a pediatrician on staff here at the hospital."

He stuck out his hand, and Grandma shook it. "Ruth Higgins. I'm Jessie's grandmother."

"I was asked to consult with you," he said.

"Could we speak in the hallway, please?" she asked.

The doctor glanced at me and nodded his head in agreement. I was rooted to the floor. When you'd dealt with crazy before, you knew to back away, and I wanted to, but I couldn't. I wouldn't leave Jessie.

With them out of the room, I wanted to try something. I approached the bed and leaned over to whisper in my sister's ear. "Lena, I know you can hear me. Slow Jessie's heart down," I pleaded. "You're killing her."

Jessie's head jerked away from me. The heart monitor continued to beep.

"Slow it down. Now!" I said.

Grandma and the doctor's mumbled conservation in the hallway increased in pace and volume. Jessie's body shuddered, and then she took a deep breath. The beeping slowed.

My muscles relaxed. Lena had heard me. Or the medicine had worked. It was one or the other.

Oh, why kid myself? It was Lena. She could control Jessie's heart rate. When Dad died, I had prayed for Lena to disappear. Those prayers went unanswered. Jessie's dissociative identity disorder was alive and well.

CHAPTER 5

BRIAN

The bright sunlight and hot air smacked me in the face I stepped out of the hospital. It was a welcome contrast to the tense, chilly hospital atmosphere.

The surrounding trees were thick with green leaves, and the smell of hot tar permeated the air in the parking lot. Grandma had sent me home to rest, but I had other ideas.

My body was stiff with tension. I rolled my shoulders to little effect. I wanted to explode. Lena's antics today would have repercussions. Anger and fear swirled around my brain like a tornado. I strode toward my car with my fists balled tightly.

Once in my car, I lowered the windows and cranked my radio. I searched my phone for a song to help me blow off some steam. "Sabotage" from the Beastie Boys pounded out of my speakers. Slamming my hands against the steering wheel, I yelled along with the lyrics. I threw my car into reverse, hit the gas, and then lunged into drive.

By the time the song ended, my tension had eased a little. Not long after, I pulled in the driveway of our well-kept, redbrick ranch-style home. Baby's eager little face greeted me as soon as I opened the front door. I leaned down and scratched her head and back.

On the short drive home, I had thought of something I needed to do. Intent on that mission, I headed to Mom and Dad's bedroom. Why hadn't Dad's fellow officers asked for his gun before or after the funeral? I shuddered to think what might've happened had Mom decided to use it in her suicide attempt instead of the pills. With Lena obviously still a factor, I needed to get the gun out of the house.

I pushed open my parents' bedroom door. Baby followed close behind. The cream walls were devoid of any decoration. The stale air smelled like unwashed sheets. My gaze settled on Dad's cherry dresser.

The top drawer slid out quietly and revealed the dull black Glock 22. A full magazine was right beside it. I gathered his gun, ammo, and badge in my black duffel bag. My stomach churned as I dug my phone out of my pocket and dialed the police station. I had to call them before I showed up and while I still had the nerve.

Sue, the dispatcher, answered the phone. "Can I speak to Detective Wheeler, please?" This is Brian Taylor, Lou's son."

"How are you, honey?" she asked.

"I'm OK," I said.

She hesitated a moment but then said, "Hang on just a minute, and I'll get the detective for you." The phone line was silent as she connected the call. Nerves on high alert, I doubted my decision to involve Detective Wheeler. I should have asked for the chief. What had I been thinking? Shit, shit, shit.

My thumb hovered over the button, but I couldn't hang up. They knew it was me.

The detective's warm, deep voice came on the line. "Hey, Brian. What can I do for you?"

"Hey, Detective. I just wanted to let someone know I was coming to the police station today to drop off my dad's gun."

"Oh, OK. I can take that from you. Just ask for me when you get here," Detective Wheeler said.

"Thanks. See you soon." I ended the call. Well, I had gotten this far. No turning back now. I dreaded talking to Detective Wheeler for any length of time. He seemed to know how to maneuver the conversation to get answers. And there were some answers I didn't want to give.

The drive to downtown Stanton was short. I parked my car and walked to the gray brick building that housed the police station. My hand sweated as I carried the duffel bag to the front counter.

"Hey, Sue. I'm here to see Detective Wheeler." I gave her a tight-lipped smile.

She studied my face. "How are you kids doing?"

"We're fine. Thank you for asking," I said. Jessie and I were always polite. We had been well trained. A few swift smacks to the head made you remember your manners.

"I'll just buzz the detective."

I shifted my weight from one foot to the other until Detective Wheeler came to get me. His presence filled the doorway. I was willing to bet he'd played football in college.

"Brian, good to see you." His big, callused hand swallowed mine. "Come right this way."

I wove through the bullpen of desks, all of them covered in papers and fast-food wrappers. The police station smelled of spicy salami sandwiches and fresh hot coffee.

All eyes were on me. I reluctantly greeted the other officers as they called out to me. Did they realize they had failed Jessie and me when we called for help two years ago? They were part of the reason why Lena had come into being.

I placed the duffel bag on the detective's desk as he shut the door. I shoved my hands in my pockets, hoping to hide the fact that I was seriously freaked out. Jessie had not been good with the detective, and to make matters worse, Lena had showed up at the funeral and talked to him. It was exactly why I should have asked for the chief.

"Have a seat," he said, settling into the chair behind his desk.

I sat down and watched as the detective unzipped the duffle bag and removed Dad's gun. He checked the gun, pulled out the ammo, and laid the badge on his desk.

"Thank you for bringing this in. We should have sent someone to pick it up already," he said.

I shrugged.

"What made you bring it in?" He leaned across his desk toward me.

I took a deep breath. I was too tired to make up any kind of story. "My mom tried to kill herself two days ago. I don't want her to use a gun if there's a next time."

His shook his head. "Oh man, I'm sorry to hear that. Is your grandmother taking care of you?"

"Yeah." Exhaustion overwhelmed me. All I wanted to do was go home and lie down. I stood up. "I need to go. Thanks for seeing me."

He reached out; his hand suspended in the space between us. "Whoa, hang on. Could you give me a few more minutes? I've been wanting to talk to you."

I swallowed. "About what?"

"It's regarding Jessie," he said.

I plopped back down and attempted a neutral expression. "What about my sister?"

"I'm concerned for you both, frankly. I've read the past report, and I know Jessie called 911 regarding your dad. No one helped you then, but I don't want to make that mistake." He rubbed the back of his neck. "The thing is your sister has demonstrated some wild behavior swings in my presence."

I bit the inside of my cheek. "I don't know what you mean. She seems like the normal level of crazy for a girl."

"Don't bullshit a bullshitter, Son. I know you know what I mean. The day we found your father's body, Jessie acted like she was a toddler or something. The day you buried your father, she came across emotionless and cold," he said.

"I don't know why she acted that way." I rubbed my face with both hands.

"I think you do know, and it would be good to talk to someone about it." His warm and caring tone coaxed me into answering.

"She has some issues, OK?" I hung my head and closed my eyes. Pushing my fear down, I told myself it would be fine to give some small details. "You would, too, if you grew up like we did."

"Did your dad chase Jessie into the woods that night?"

Bam. There it was: the million-dollar question. I couldn't believe he'd asked it, but clearly, he'd figured out why my dad had been in the woods. He watched my face as I tried to form an answer.

"Are you blaming my sister?" I could barely get the words out.

He sighed. "No. And besides, your dad's case has already been ruled an accidental death."

My eyes locked with his. I had learned to read people, and I trusted him. The case was closed. Maybe I was making a huge mistake, but I prayed I was right.

"Do I have your word you won't put her in jail?" I asked.

"You have my word," he said as he scooted his chair forward.

"Before Dad's death, you know we were in a car accident, right? Brian said.

Detective Wheeler nodded quickly.

"While Mom and I were in the hospital, Jessie told Mom that Dad was drinking again. Mom confronted Dad about it." I wiped the sweat from my upper lip. My right eye had begun to twitch, which I desperately hoped he didn't notice.

Trying to avoid direct eye contact, I stared out the window. The sunny day was a stark contrast to my current conversation.

I should have buried the gun in the backyard.

"I guess Dad left the hospital and got drunk. He tried to choke Jessie when he got home, but she hit him with a candlestick and ran away."

The detective nodded his head vigorously. "I'd wondered how he'd broken his finger on his left hand."

I swallowed hard. That little detail made me sick. Lena had told me she'd hit Dad with a candlestick. Detective Wheeler's observation made her story undeniable. I'd held onto a shred of hope that my father wouldn't have killed her, but not anymore. If Lena was telling the truth about fighting back, then she was telling the truth about his threatening actions.

I took a deep breath and continued. "She ran for the woods because she didn't think he would follow her, but he did. You already know how it ended."

He nodded his head in confirmation and drummed his fingers on his desk. "Did your sister know about the hole in the woods?" he said.

Would he pin premediated murder on my sister if I answered yes? Jessie knew the hole was there, which meant Lena did too. But she didn't push him into it.

The full weight of the moment hit me. Being completely honest was all I could do. I didn't know how to spin a story around the events of that night.

"Yeah, we dug it with a bunch of our friends. It was our foxhole for war games." I glanced at him quickly. Oh yeah, he was watching me closely.

"I wondered how it got there. Do you think he would have killed her?" he said.

"Yes, I do," I said slowly and deliberately. "He couldn't control himself."

"Some things just never end," he said, shaking his head and pulling his shirt collar away from his neck. He cast his eyes down at the desk like he was lost in thought. After a few breaths, he pushed his chair away from the desk and met my gaze. "I want you to know that my father was like yours. I understand what you're saying."

A weight lifted from my chest. I had been right about him. It was such a relief. I wasn't afraid that I had just admitted this to someone.

I scrubbed my face with my hands. "Am I good to go?"

"Just one more thing. Jessie needs counseling. She obviously has some big issues to work through. Make sure it happens," he said.

"I will," I said.

"You may not understand this now, but when you get older, you'll need to work through the issues of your past." His deep brown eyes locked with mine, and I nodded. "Should I talk to your grandmother about it?"

"No, I will tell her," I said. He would follow up; this wasn't idle talk.

He nodded and waved me out the door. Well, that was it. Our secret was out. My stomach sank. I would have to tell Grandma the essential details. And the worst part: I had to betray my sister to help her.

CHAPTER 6

BRIAN

The following day, Jessie was released from the hospital. Her heart rate had stayed in the normal range. I paced back and forth in front of our bay window, waiting for her and Grandma to come home. Baby's big, brown eyes watched me from her perch on the couch.

I tried to psych myself up for the difficult task ahead. "Baby, when Jessie gets here, I need to you to give her lots of attention."

Baby eagerly wagged her tail in agreement. I rubbed her head. She would be another thing I would miss at college. School seemed very far away right now, but the thought of leaving in the fall gave me pause. I had a hard enough time thinking about leaving Tracey. How in the hell could I go away with all this happening?

Grandma's car pulled into the driveway. I rolled my shoulders back, trying to release the tension. The talk had to happen today, or it wouldn't happen at all. I would tell them most of the story at the same time.

A door in the kitchen opened, and Grandma and Jessie filed in from the garage.

"Hey, how's it going?" I said nervously, distributing my weight from one foot to the other.

"I'm glad to be home. Let's just keep it at that," Jessie said. Baby ran to Jessie for her fill of hugs and kisses.

"I bet. So, what did the doctor say? Any follow-up?" I said.

Jessie met my gaze briefly and then lowered her eyes. She put her bag down on the kitchen counter. "I have to do mandatory counseling per Mom's psychiatrist," she said quietly.

Relief flooded through me. Part of my job was done. At least I didn't have to push for counseling. And Jessie needed it.

I couldn't resist making a joke. "Well, you *did* twist his nuts," I said with a nervous laugh.

"Brian!" Grandma gasped.

Jessie burst out laughing, and I joined her. We both doubled over, clutching our stomachs. We always laughed at the same stupid shit— especially in stressful situations.

After a few minutes, I pulled myself together. "Um, could the two of you sit down for a minute? I wanted to talk to you about what happened at the hospital."

Grandma, who had been making coffee, quickly turned to stare at me. Her brows pulled together into a deep frown, and her eyes searched my face.

"Why?" Jessie said. She stopped petting Baby and gaped at me. If she was trying to make me squirm, it was working.

"We can do that," Grandma said, maintaining a neutral tone of voice. "Let me just finish making coffee."

Jessie and I sat down at the dining room table. Jessie mouthed, "What are you doing?" Her faced was creased with worry.

"Cool it," I whispered with a quick shake of my head.

Grandma set cups of coffee in front of us. Her lips were pressed into a tight line as she sat across from me.

"I have to tell Grandma about what's going on. It can't just be between you and me any longer," I said.

The color drained from Jessie's face. My hand reflexively reached toward her in a calming gesture. She had to know I wouldn't hurt her intentionally.

Jessie took a deep breath.

"What's going on? Brian, you're scaring me," Grandma said.

In a stroke of genius, I thought of someone who could explain what was going on with Jessie better than I. Someone who had talked to Lena, however briefly.

"I'm sorry. I'm not trying to scare you. I think you should contact our school counselor, Mrs. Palmer. She called once last year and asked for a meeting, but Dad blew up at Jessie. I don't think Mom ever called Mrs. Palmer back," I said.

Grandma dropped her head into her hands. "Going forward, no matter what happens, you have to tell me. I'm here to help you," she said, reaching for Jessie's hand and maintaining eye contact with me.

Jessie and I looked at each other and then back to Grandma. We each gave a firm nod.

"OK," I said.

Grandma's shoulders relaxed a bit. Her gaze switched to Jessie. "Why did the counselor want to contact your mom?"

Jessie slumped over her coffee. "I talked to her a little bit about the stress and fighting at home and how it was affecting me. She wanted Mom and Dad to come in and talk about it, but like Brian said, Dad lost his mind over it. Since I worked in the office, I accessed my files, and I changed our phone number so she couldn't call again. We hid the letters."

"OK..." Grandma raised her brows.

"It's called survival," Jessie said quietly.

"I don't blame you, sweetheart," Grandma said. She twisted her wedding ring around her finger. "I'm glad you told me. I will try and contact her now, but I may not get ahold of her until school starts. In the meantime, your mom's psychiatrist has insisted Jessie attend six weeks of outpatient counseling at the Oaks."

My mouth dropped open. Holy shit. He wasn't fooling around. I had heard of kids going there for eating disorders, drug problems, and other issues. It was an intense place.

"There goes my summer," Jessie mumbled. She absently picked up the spoon for her coffee and dropped it on the cloth place mat.

Grandma reached across the table again and squeezed our hands. "It's important that the two of you talk to a professional about what you've been through." She studied my face. "Brian, is there something else?"

"Yeah," I said, pushing my hair off my forehead. "I'm sorry, Jess, but I have to tell Grandma."

Jessie's head snapped up, and her mouth dropped open.

Time to jump into the deep end of the pool. "You know how Jessie doesn't remember attacking Mom's doctor?" I said.

Grandma nodded.

"I also saw her get into a fight with a girl at school, and she doesn't remember it either," I said. "There are other memory gaps. Her therapist will need to know."

Grandma's face drained of color. This was going super well.

"I'm glad you told me," she said, taking a deep breath.

"Are we finished talking about all my emotional issues now?" Jessie said. While she wasn't the ball of nerves she'd been moments ago, her cheeks were pink with embarrassment.

"Jessie, it will be all right. We'll figure it out," Grandma said.

Jessie hung her head. "OK. Can I go take a shower now? I want to wash the hospital stink off."

"Of course," Grandma said as she reached for our empty coffee cups.

Jessie hung her head and walked toward the hallway. I followed and tapped her arm before she could escape into the bathroom.

"Why did you do that?" she said quietly.

"I had to. It's getting out of control. We need help," I said.

Her eyes began to tear, and her bottom lip quivered. "You mean I need help." She pulled her arm away from me. "Just go."

Reluctantly, I stepped back. She hurried into the bathroom and closed the door in my face. I anxiously stood outside the bathroom door and listened. The only sound was the drum of the shower. I would wait until we were alone to tell her about Lena and the little girl. I just couldn't go into the detail with Grandma yet. I owed Jessie all the information first.

CHAPTER 7

JESSIE

I vigorously toweled my hair dry. Thank God I was still allowed to go out with Will tonight. After the past week, I desperately needed a break from all the serious discussions. Honestly, I was amazed he wanted to go out with me after all he had witnessed. Maybe it was a sympathy date.

The thought stopped me cold, and I stared at my reflection in our bathroom mirror. I let doubt run wild, but my gut said that wasn't the reason he'd asked me out. My muscles relaxed. That was a relief. A night out with Will was just what I wanted. Typical teen girl stuff.

An hour later, my hair and makeup complete, I was ready to go. The low rumble of a car pulling into our driveway alerted me to Will's arrival. A black Jeep gleamed in the evening light. Of course Will would own a Jeep. It was a great match for his easygoing, outdoorsy vibe.

"Bye, Grandma. Will's here to pick me up. I'll be back by eleven." I grabbed my phone and purse and ran out the front door before Grandma or Brian could comment.

The evening was perfect. Riding around in the open air was just what I wanted. A warm breeze lifted my hair and caressed my freshly shaved, bare legs. We pulled into Stanton River Park, which bordered the Stanton River. Will switched off the car but left the radio playing "Time Machine" by Willow.

I smiled at Will. "Good song," I said.

Without thinking about it, I started to sing along with the chorus. "Please don't wait on me, on me."

"You have a great voice. Seriously," Will said as the song ended.

"Thanks. I love to sing. I made the school choir," I said, a little proud about it.

"I hear why," Will said, smiling back at me.

We sat by the river, talking and listening to music. Being out and having fun was such a welcome change. It was just what my soul craved.

His long arm bridged the distance between our seats and his hand found mine. My heart melted as our fingers wove together. I held his hand in my lap.

Did he plan our evening together? If so, I was impressed. I squeezed his hand and relaxed my head against the seat. I couldn't remember the last time I was so at peace. I wanted to forget all the trauma of the past few weeks.

"Do you want to walk over to Poppy's for ice cream?" Will said.

"You know it," I said. Another masterstroke on Will's part; the way to my heart was paved in chocolate.

Ice cream cones purchased; we strolled the Riverwalk. My chocolate almond fudge ice cream melted on my tongue and quickly disappeared.

"I think I could eat five of these," I said as I swallowed the last bite.

"I know, right?" Will nodded. "Do you want to go back for some fries?"

"Absolutely" I said, smiling.

Will did an immediate about-face, amid my giggles, and we headed back to Poppy's. We sat down at the picnic tables with our hot, lightly salted fries and little cups of ketchup.

"The perfect dinner," I said.

"Fattening foods are the best," Will said. We each held up a fry and clinked them together in a toast. A comfortable silence descended as we chowed down on our fries. Once I had finished, I wiped the salt and ketchup from my hands and smiled at Will.

"Do you want to walk along the river again?" he asked.

"Yeah, that sounds good," I said. Will got up from the table and held his hand out to me. I happily took it, and we walked back along the Riverwalk.

"How are you doing with your mom and everything?" he asked.

I met his intense gaze. He really wanted to know how I was; this wasn't just polite conversation. I resigned myself to reliving it a bit to give him the answer he deserved.

"It's been hard," I said. "I'm angry at her. I'm sad she would do that to herself. It's just hard to even understand why she would do it."

"Yeah, I don't get it either," he said, squeezing my hand gently. "I wish I could help you."

His words, his good intentions, brought tears to my eyes. I smiled sadly up at him. "You have—you are. You stayed with me that night. You ran back into a house with a screaming girl. Most people would have called 911 and then run away," I said. "Thank you."

I had wanted to thank him but hadn't been sure how to start the conversation. Of course, he had done it for me.

Will stopped walking and faced me directly. "I will always help you. I mean it. If you need anything, I want you to call me," he said.

I nodded. There was still so much I could tell him, but I didn't want to talk about my serious problems. It was too much to deal with. I didn't trust myself to speak, as I didn't want to start ugly crying.

Will was a keeper, no question. Taking a minute to get ahold of my emotions, I rummaged around in my small purse and found some mint gum.

"Want some?" I held out a stick.

"Yeah, thanks."

Hopefully, the gum would get rid of any bits of french fry stuck in my teeth. We walked back to Will's Jeep hand in hand.

The late summer sun was setting, and the sky glowed with purple and pink clouds. Will stopped by the passenger door and stood directly in front of me. I let go of his hand and wrapped my arms around his waist. My head rested on his chest, and I breathed in his fresh, clean smell. He wrapped his arms around my shoulders and kissed the top of my head. Tilting my face up, I invited his kiss.

His soft, plump lips pressed to mine as his fingers caressed my jaw. I was drowning in sweet sensation. His kiss followed my lead. There was nothing in the world I would have rather been doing.

We broke apart, and Will rested his forehead against mine. I smiled up at him.

"Oh, hang on a sec," I said, pulling away. I still had gum in my mouth. Before the kissing continued, I'd need to get rid of it.

Where was a trash can when you needed one? Small, green shrubs bordered the parking lot. I aimed for the dark-brown mulch beneath them and spit. My gum arced upward and then dropped conveniently into the mulch.

"I can't believe you just did that," Will said. His burst of laughter brought me to my senses.

My cheeks flushed with heat. "I'm so sorry. I lapsed into Brian behavior. We used to have spitting contests for distance and accuracy. Just with gum though. Loogies are gross."

"Good thing you made that distinction," Will said, laughing.

"You should try it. Can you spit gum that far?" I said, forgetting my embarrassment.

"Um, no. I haven't had the hours of practice you've clearly had." His eyes crinkled upward with his smile.

"Right." I nodded.

Will took me in his arms and squeezed, a chuckle rumbled up his throat. The absence of judgement put me at ease, and I leaned into him. Our relationship was different from the one I'd had with Alex. I was myself with Will. Why was I surprised he wanted to get to know me?

"Let's get you home. I don't want to ruin my good standing with Brian." Will opened the car door for me, and I climbed in. I loved how he treated me like a queen.

He confidently maneuvered the Jeep out of the parking lot and back onto the main road, the muscles in his long arms flexing with each turn. He looked good driving. Honestly, he looked good no matter what he was doing.

We held hands, and I watched the dark cornfields roll by. "Knee high by July" was the saying for corn, and the fields appeared to be right on schedule. They faded into the distance as we hooked a left into my neighborhood. We pulled into the driveway, greeted by the glow of the living room lights—a sign Grandma had waited up for me.

Will put the car in park. "Want to hang out later this week?"

"Yeah, maybe at the pool on Saturday? Rebecca and I were planning to go," I said.

"Sounds good." He leaned over and kissed me with his impossibly soft lips. Dazed, happy and humming softly, I floated to my front door.

CHAPTER 8

JESSIE

The Oaks wellness center had large, tinted windows overlooking the grounds. As it was my first day here, I appreciated the calming atmosphere. The place was a smaller version of a hospital—not my favorite—but at least the garden was nice to look at. The surrounding lawns were a lush green, with pink rosebushes dotting the landscape. Yellow sunflowers filled the flower beds.

Because of my outburst with Mom's doctor, I was now attending outpatient group counseling for six weeks *and* individual weekly counseling. Thank God I wasn't forced to do inpatient care. That was comparable to a hospital stay, and it scared me to death. I didn't want to be trapped somewhere with no way to escape.

Mom's doctor had insisted on counseling so he wouldn't feel compelled to press charges for what I had done. Brian had filled me in on the gory details. I was embarrassed and uncomfortable with what I had done. But the familiar rage still swirled in my gut. No one had to tell me my emotional health was precarious. Psychologically I was on a rocky ledge peering into a vast canyon. Just one puff of air, and I would be gone.

I rolled the number two pencil between my fingers and thought about what to write. It was our reflection time. A time to put our thoughts and feelings on paper. My newly purchased journal, with its black, glossy cover, awaited me. I decided to just write whatever came to mind and see where it took me.

Dear journal,

This place is OK so far, but I have no idea if any of it will help! Ding-dong, the witch is dead. Well, not really a witch, but my dad is dead. And for that, I'm grateful. At least now I don't have to constantly be on guard in my own home. My mom is needy and annoying but still way better than having Dad around. If there's a hell, Dad, you're in it. I hope you enjoy the eternal inferno that is your new home. That line makes me laugh. I hope he's scared wherever he is. It's payback time.

Thinking of evil, I also want my archenemy, Amanda, to have a horrible summer and suffer from some incurable venereal disease. Now that really makes me smile. Since my ex-boyfriend, Alex, slept with her, I hope he has the same disease. I pray they both have such big, inflamed pustules on their privates that it hurts to pee. Forget about sex entirely! I want them to stay indoors all summer just to keep their irritated areas cool and pain free. I imagine them sitting naked in front of a fan, airing themselves for hours each day and clinging to a desperate desire for the pustules to heal. Talk about a visual I really don't want. I crack myself up!

Hey, writing this is fun. Maybe there is something to this exercise.

OK, let's focus on other topics. I've been watching so much of The Crown on Netflix my internal dialogue has a British accent!

Watching The Crown is something Mom and I do together now. It's kind of nice. She rubs my feet while we watch. At the same time, it's weird to have her attention now that Dad's gone.

But forget The Crown. What I would really like to be doing right now is hanging at the pool with Rebecca, eating Twizzlers, and getting a tan. Rebecca and I are going to train to be lifeguards, so next summer, I'll practically live at the pool.

Talk to you later, journal.

I tried to pay attention as Dan, one of the therapists, wrapped up our group session. Three other kids with various issues made up our group. Greg had anxiety, Kylie dealt with depression, I obviously had many issues—anger, losing time, and attacking people, to name a few—and Matt was conflicted about being gay. None of them went to school with me, which was a relief. Embarrassment made me want to shrink into a very small version of myself.

"That's it for today. Remember to bring your folders, and we'll focus on coping mechanisms tomorrow morning," Dan said. We scattered quickly.

I squinted against the late-afternoon sun, looking for Brian's car in the parking lot. His hand shot out of his open window and waved at me. I wished Grandma had come to pick me up. Brian's loose lips had the potential to make my situation a hundred times worse.

"Hey," I said as I grudgingly got into the car.

"Hey, how'd it go?" He fidgeted with his hands in his lap. His right fist ground against the palm of his left hand.

He turned in his seat to make eye contact, but I slid my gaze forward. "It was great. I love counseling," I said.

He sighed. "I know you're upset, but I didn't have any other options,"

"Uh-huh," I said. He was right. My actions landed me in therapy, not his. And all of this *was* pretty scary. Which was probably why I jumped at the chance to pout about something.

"Jess, I need to tell you a couple things, and then you can decide if you want to share them with anyone else."

"OK." I looked over at him warily.

"You know the day you attacked Amanda?" he said.

"Yes, I remember what you told me." This was one attack that didn't bother me. I hated Amanda with a passion. Brian had told me that I'd thrown a hot dog at her in the lunchroom and threatened her. I smiled slightly. It sounded epic.

"And remember when Mrs. Palmer mentioned you had symptoms of dissociative identity disorder?"

"Yeah," I said, frowning.

"It's OK," he said, motioning with his hands for me to remain calm. "I think you do have it. That day, after you threatened Amanda, your other personality talked to me. She told me her name was Lena."

"Oh my God," I said, my eyes going wide. "You talked to my other personality, and she has a different name?"

Shocked, I remembered a time while Dad was missing when Brian had called me Lena and asked me a question.

"Yeah," he said, releasing a big breath.

"Did Lena kill Dad?" I asked with bated breath. The hair on the back of my neck stood on end.

"No, but he tried to choke her. She got away from him and ran for the woods. She led him to the foxhole and jumped over. He fell in," he said.

My mind raced. Images of the woods and the foxhole flashed through my brain.

"What was she like? What did she say?" I whispered.

"She said she came to protect us. To protect us from Dad." His face looked worn with concern.

"I talked to one more personality too," he said. "The day we found Dad dead, you seemed like a little girl. You talked like you were very young and put your thumb in your mouth."

Emotionally, I was free-falling into a dark canyon with no bottom in sight. It was too much. "I can't handle this," I sobbed. "I can't."

Brian gripped my shoulder. "I will help you; Grandma will help you. You aren't alone in this."

I turned my head, tears running down my face, and stared blankly out the window. Internally, I prayed. *God, please help me.* Even with all I had been through, my mental state scared me the most.

CHAPTER 9

JESSIE

The next day, I was back at the Oaks, waiting in a private office. From the light-blue walls hung a few generic mindfulness quotes framed in white. This must have been a shared space; it had no personality.

I jiggled my left leg incessantly. Grandma gently put her hand on my knee.

"I know. I can't stop wiggling," I said. Dread loomed within me, just waiting for the next opportunity to overtake me.

There was a light knock on the door, and Mrs. Palmer, dressed in a summery, pale-yellow pantsuit, rushed in. She laid her purse and papers on the floor, then extended her hand to Grandma. "I'm Mrs. Palmer, Jessie's guidance counselor.

"It's nice to meet you," Grandma said.

Mrs. Palmer's concerned gaze met my wary one. "Jessie," she said, her face lined with worry. "Can I give you a hug?"

"Of course," I said with a nod. She wrapped her arms around me and patted my upper back. Her fresh floral scent enveloped me. I was safe with her; she was on my side.

"I'm so sorry you've been through all this," she said, taking a seat next to me. "I wanted to reach out to you, but I wasn't sure if I should."

Grandma straightened in her seat. "I do have a question about why you didn't report the suspected abuse to the authorities."

My jaw dropped. Leave it to Grandma to cut to the chase.

"Grandma!" I exclaimed.

"No, it's OK." Mrs. Palmer straightened her suit jacket. "I understand why you're asking me, and I've thought about it a lot. Jessie only told me her parents argued and yelled. When I questioned her, she didn't indicate any verbal or physical abuse."

Grandma nodded her head. "I see." The stern set of Grandma's jaw told me she wasn't going to let Mrs. Palmer off the hook easily.

"Jessie's so good at hiding her situation. I didn't pick up on it until just before her father went missing," she said. She sucked her lips between her teeth.

"Why then?" Grandma asked.

Mrs. Palmer took a deep breath and met my gaze with concern. "I saw an altercation between Jessie and another student. I talked with Jessie about it afterward, and she was so different in her manner and speech I realized she needed help."

Grandma frowned. "What do mean she was different in manner and speech?"

"When I first met Jessie last year, she described an event to me where she was very disoriented. In her words, she was disconnected from her body. This worried me, as it appeared to be a serious reaction to stress in her home. And as I mentioned, I became more concerned when I talked with her after the incident. Her personality was vastly different. It seemed like a complete disconnect from who I know Jessie to be."

Several imagined violent scenes flitted through my mind. I wished I could disappear.

Grandma's hand pressed against her heart. "Jessie, is that true?"

"I don't remember the fight with Amanda," I said softly.

Grandma grabbed my hand. Her lips turned downward.

"What's going to happen?" I said, clearing my throat. Cold chills crept up my back, and I started to tremble.

"With your grandmother's permission, I've talked with the counselors here about what you told me and what I observed." She took a deep breath. "I've recommended a colleague of mine to counsel you. Her name is Dr. Chen. She's a great doctor and shares a similar background to yours," she said.

"I thought you would counsel me." My chest tightened painfully, and I slumped in my chair, fighting the urge to curl in a ball. I didn't want to meet yet another counselor and discuss my issues.

"I'm sorry. I wish I could, but I don't have the training or the experience in the type of counseling you need," she said gently.

I wrapped my arms around myself and rested my forehead against my knees. My body shook uncontrollably.

"Jessie, what's wrong?" Mrs. Palmer's voice was anxious and high pitched.

My jaw had locked, but I forced out the words. "I'm cold."

Mrs. Palmer flew out of her seat and jerked open the door. "I need some help in here, please!"

A nurse wearing green Crocs and scrubs approached me. She wrapped a thin hospital blanket around my shoulders, then she and Mrs. Palmer eased me into a wheelchair. I tried to shrink further down into the blanket. I wondered where I was going but was too cold and tired to ask.

Moments later, I was lying in a hospital bed beneath a warm blanket. I closed my eyes. A nurse gently extracted my arm from the blankets and took my blood pressure and heart rate.

"Her blood pressure is too low," she said to Grandma. "She may be in shock. "I'm going to insert an IV. The fluids will get her blood pressure up."

I winced as a needle slid into my arm. *Ugh, not another IV.* My arms were going to look like I was shooting heroin or something.

"Don't," I said, trying to pull my arm back. But the nurse held it firmly. Grandma's hand gently squeezed my shoulder. I let go and allowed my mind and body to drift into sleep.

CHAPTER 10

BRIAN

A week had passed since Jessie's breakdown at the Oaks, and this was the first chance I'd had to see Tracey. I needed to give her the dirty details on our family and Jessie's issues. I wanted her support.

I stood in the garage as I put my arms over my head and tried to stretch out my tense back. My summer break was coming to an end.

I was leaving for Miami University in Oxford, Ohio, in a month, and Tracey was headed for Bowling Green, also in Ohio. She wanted to be a journalism major, and I was going into business administration. We would be about three hours apart. Not too far, but far enough that we would have to plan our visits.

Tracey pulled up in front of our house and parked on the street so she wouldn't block the driveway. I waved to her from the garage, grabbed a couple dusty fishing poles, and trotted out to my car to load them into the back of my trunk. I tipped my head back and let the sun wash over my face.

It was a relief to do something simple and fun with Tracey. I was a little nervous about filling her in on Jessie, as her issues were pretty mind-blowing, but I also trusted that she would support me.

I watched as Tracey walked toward me. Smiling, shoulders relaxed, she looked great. I liked seeing her happy. It had been a rough few months when she miscarried. Somehow, I had made my peace with the loss.

We would have our baby when the time was right. I had been googling stuff on miscarriages, and this spiritual-based article by some doctor had come up. I started reading and found it fascinating. It said you're meant to have the babies that come to you. If the baby doesn't survive, it will come back again when the time is right. It made sense. I showed the article to Tracey, but she wasn't sure if that was how it worked.

She would be my wife and the mother of my children someday. Our connection was so gut level and deep, I had no doubts.

We kept the car windows rolled down as we left the subdivision and drove the back roads past soft, rolling hills. The houses soon disappeared, and farmland surrounded us.

At the top of the next hill, we pulled up to the Grant Park security hut. An older, gray-haired guy walked sedately over to my window and checked my membership card, which I got for free as a family member of a Stanton police officer. Or, I guess, a former officer.

He waved me through as the security gate lifted. The expanse of the park unfolded around us. The enormous man-made lake nestled in a valley and reached far into the surrounding woods. You could disappear in the park, with its thick green canopy of trees and many hidden trails.

We slowly drove to my favorite fishing spot, the smell of hot dogs sizzling on the grill catching my attention. The snack shop was open. My mouth started to water. Hot dogs with mustard were one of my favorite lunches, along with burritos.

"Hey, do you want to stop and get some hot dogs?" I said, delaying our important chat a little.

It was a rhetorical question, as we both knew we were stopping to eat. Tracey chuckled.

"I figured we'd be stopping as soon as I smelled the grill," she said. She reached over and gently squeezed the back of my neck. I grabbed her hand and kissed her palm.

I parked the car, and we walked over to the snack shop. The whole park appeared to be staffed by retired guys. A short, bald, and big-bellied man wearing a striped, green apron worked the grill and turned the jumbo hot dogs with tongs. A white, open-sided tent shaded him from the hot noonday sun.

"Good afternoon," he said as we approached.

"Good afternoon," I said in return. I dug my wallet from the back pocket of my shorts and pulled out a twenty-dollar bill.

"We'll take three hot dogs, two Cokes, and a bottle of water, please."

"You bet," he answered. He wrapped the hot dogs in tinfoil and handed them to me in a plastic bag. He dug into the ice-filled cooler and pulled out two cans of Coke and one bottle of water. He added those to a second plastic bag.

With our lunch in tow, we made our way to a shaded part of the shoreline so we could put our blanket down. Tracey spread a large, multicolored quilt on the ground and set out our food. I stared out at the lake as I devoured my hot dog. The water lapped gently against the shore, and a light breeze made it comfortable.

"How's Jessie doing?" Tracey asked.

Frowning, I swallowed my last bite. "She's OK, I guess. She's anxious about going to therapy at the Oaks."

"Yeah, that makes sense, but I'm glad she's getting counseling. She hasn't seemed like herself at times over the last year," she said.

I stared down at the quilt. She had given me the perfect opening.

"I think so too." I took a deep breath. "I need to tell you what's really going on with her."

Picking up on my distress, Tracey scooted closer to me and put her hand on my back. Her brow wrinkled. "What's wrong?"

"Please don't be upset that I haven't told you this before, OK?" I pleaded briefly while meeting her steady gaze.

"OK," she said slowly.

"I haven't told anyone about this, except recently Grandma. And that was only because I had to."

Tracey nodded her head in encouragement.

"Anyway, you know I thought my dad was a jerk, but it was a lot worse than that. He was violent. He would push Mom around, and if Jessie or I tried to intervene, he would hit us too. He would hit Jessie and me for the stupidest shit. It made no sense."

The scene of Dad smacking Jessie in the head ran through my mind. Jessie's legs had buckled after the blow. I hated him for it. I rubbed my fist against my left palm until Tracey placed her hand over mine.

"That's awful. I'm so sorry," Tracey said, her eyebrows drawing together. "Didn't your mom try to stop him?"

"She would try and get in between, but it didn't matter. He would still hit us. The abuse caused a lot of emotional issues with Jessie," I said, meeting Tracey's concerned gaze. "I think she has dissociative identity disorder. Mrs. Palmer, our high school guidance counselor, thinks she does too."

I pressed my lips together, waiting for Tracey's reaction.

"Wow, that's a lot of information," Tracey said, rubbing her forehead.

"I know. I had to talk to someone though. It's just too much to handle," I said.

"I'm glad you told me. The way she's been acting makes more sense now," Tracey said. "Let's walk. I feel like I need to move."

"Yeah, OK," I said. We rose from the quilt and headed toward one of the nearby walking trails.

"Why do you think she has a dissociative disorder?" Tracey asked.

"She gets really mean, and it's so unlike her. She doesn't remember when she acts that way either. She threatened Dad with a knife," I said.

"Oh my God! What did he do?" Tracey stumbled. I reached out my hand to steady her.

"We were at my grandma's, and luckily she intervened. I don't even want to think about what could have happened," I said.

"I'm not mad at you, but how did you not tell me about this?" Tracey stared at me with wide eyes.

"I don't know," I said, shaking my head. "I didn't want to talk about how bad it was at home."

She nodded and stared absently at the forest floor. The canopy of trees shielded us from the sun and cast shadows over her solemn eyes. It was cooler in the woods, and despite the serious conversation, I felt my shoulders relax. Just being in nature made me calmer.

"Why does Mrs. Palmer think she has the disorder?" Tracey said.

"She saw the fight between Jessie and Amanda in the cafeteria, and she talked to Jessie afterward. She noticed how different Jessie acted. At that point, Jessie had already told her about the fighting at home and how it was stressing her out. She kind of put the pieces together," I said.

Tracey stopped. Her arms snaked around my shoulders and pulled me into a hug. I rested my head against hers.

"I don't want to think about not seeing you for months at a time," I whispered.

"I know," she whispered before pressing her lips to mine. "We'll get through it."

Her green eyes locked with mine. My chest squeezed painfully just thinking about it. Tracey squeezed me tighter. "We won't be too far apart. Just think of the fun road trips we'll have visiting each other."

I let her comfort me. Where it seemed like everything sucked, she was my rock. We ambled down the wooded path, our fingers entwined between us.

CHAPTER 11

JESSIE

An unnerving blue-gray light filled my home. My skin prickled with cold. All my nightmares lived here. I could feel a pull to Brian's room, but he wasn't there. Something else demanded my attention. Deep down, I knew it was the same sinister shape I'd seen before. I couldn't run from it. I had to see. I needed to know what it wanted.

I stopped in Brian's doorway. Instead of the ominous black swirl, I found a translucent boy. He paced back and forth with a scowl on his face. I blinked, but he was still there.

He didn't seem to notice me as I took him in. He was older than I'd originally thought—a teenager, most likely. Tall and slim, he had a mop of dark-brown hair. I could see Brian's bed through him.

I stepped into the room. "Who are you?"

Hissing, he drew his lips back from his teeth. "This is your fault," he said.

A wall of rage crashed over me, and I crumpled to my knees. He lunged toward me, pushing me backward. His hateful face was inches from mine. I tried to push him away. He was cold and damp, but there was no substance to him, nothing for me to scratch or push against. My hands slid through him. His cold hands wrapped around my throat.

"Stop!" I gasped. "What are you doing?" I clawed at my throat, try-ing to break his hold but still incapable of touching his insubstantial form. I got my feet under me and forcibly pushed myself away. I couldn't move his body, but I could move mine. My push broke his hold, and I scrambled backward.

"You won't get away this time," he said and smiled.

I got to my feet and lunged toward the front door. His cold weight covered my back and his hands wrapped around my neck again. I struggled to move forward to break his hold. Black dots narrowed my vision. I couldn't breathe. I was losing this fight.

My body jerked into consciousness. My heart pounded as I took a huge breath. It was just a dream.

"Jessie?" Grandma said near me. Her soft hand covered mine.

I blinked to clear my vision. The room was dim, but the tinges of pink and purple coming through the window indicated the sun had set. Panic surged through me. I turned toward Grandma.

"Don't leave me here overnight," I said.

"No, honey. I won't. I'll take you home as soon as the doctor checks you out," she said.

I searched her lined, tired face. Her mouth was turned down. I was causing her too much stress.

"I'm sorry. I don't know what's wrong with me," I said, grabbing the hospital bed remote and raising my bed to a sitting position.

"There is nothing wrong with you. You've been through too much," Grandma said as she patted my hand.

"Hey," Brian said as he walked in the room. His gaze was assessing, but I must have looked OK since he came over to me. He leaned close. "You must love hospital beds."

"Shut up." I smacked his arm. "You're not funny." I gripped the thin and slightly scratchy hospital blanket to my chest.

"Brian!" Grandma admonished him.

His comments did make me wonder why this kept happening. Why was he fine, but I was losing it? I made a mental note to ask my counselor.

Regardless of his stupid comments, I was more at ease when he was around.

Dr. Anderson, one of the center's doctors, strode into the room. I recognized her from our meetings. I guessed she was in her forties. She had well-defined lines around her kind eyes.

"Hello, I'm glad to see you awake and sitting up. How're you feeling?" she said.

"I feel fine now," I said.

"And how did you feel earlier, before this happened?" she asked.

"Upset and scared." I sighed. "I had hoped Mrs. Palmer would be my counselor."

"That's understandable," she said, reaching out and squeezing my hand gently. "I think you experienced nonmedical shock, which is a response to anxiety or fear. The symptoms mimic medical shock. You had a fight-or-flight type of reaction, but it's short lived, and symptoms usually resolve once the person is comforted."

Grandma listened intently to Dr. Anderson and nodded her head. I was just relieved it was over.

"That makes sense. Jessie has had to deal with a lot lately," Grandma said.

The doctor murmured her assent and turned to me. "I'm going to release you now to go home. Your blood pressure and temperature are normal. Rest tomorrow and make sure to drink enough water."

"She will. Thank you, Doctor," Grandma said.

I was all good with Grandma answering for me. She handed me a sweatshirt to put over my T-shirt. I took it gladly. It was cold in the building, and the fear from my dream still lingered.

"Brian, why don't you take Jessie home. I need to pick up my medication at the pharmacy," Grandma said.

"Sure, no problem," Brian said.

Thirty minutes later, with music blaring, Brian and I pulled into our driveway. My stomach churned just looking at the house.

"What's wrong?" Brian asked. "You're making the dread face."

Of course my brother would recognize my dread. He'd seen this expression on my face each time we faced the looming presence of our dad.

"Twice I've had this horrible nightmare about a ghost or something in your room. It tried to kill me both times. First it was a black swirl of fog, and then in the second dream, it was a teenage boy, but I could see through him," I said.

"I'm not trying to kill you." Brian frowned and shook his head.

"No, it's not you. I know that. He's tall and thin with a lot of dark hair," I said.

"Come on, it's just a stress dream. You have to learn how to relax," he said.

I sighed and rubbed my forehead. "I know."

"If you have the dream again, wake yourself up. Remember it's just a dream. That's what I do," Brian said. "A dream isn't going to kill you."

"If you say so," I said.

CHAPTER 12

JESSIE

S unlight streamed through the cracks in my curtains. My pool date was a go. I scrambled out of bed and pulled my curtains aside. A beautiful, clear blue sky showed overhead, and a smile stretched across my face. I opened my bedroom door and listened. Grandma's light steps moved over the creaking linoleum floor in the kitchen. The smell of bacon filled the air. On my left, Brian's door was closed, so I assumed he was still asleep.

Surveillance complete, I went to the bathroom and locked the door. I didn't need to be on guard all the time anymore, but my self-preservation instinct was alive and well. I turned on the shower, undressed, and stepped under the hot spray. I shaved my legs carefully. My pale skin practically glowed. *Crap.* I needed some sun. I worked conditioner into the ends of my fuzz-prone hair, then rinsed.

When I leaned down to turn the water off, the light went out. I quickly straightened and peeked around the shower curtain. My brow furrowed. Brian wasn't there. Typically, he would flush the toilet as his next trick.

"Brian!" I yelled. I grabbed my towel off the rack and wrapped it around myself. The small window above the shower provided enough light for me to peer at the light switch. It was in the down position—off.

The door was still locked from the inside. Chill bumps erupted all over my body.

Frowning, I flipped the switch. Light flooded the bathroom, but it didn't calm my nerves. I unsteadily put on my T-shirt and shorts and jerked the bathroom door open.

I stomped into the kitchen. Grandma stood with her back to me, cooking on the stove top. Brian wasn't in the kitchen.

"Hey, Grandma, where's Brian?" I said.

"Good morning, sweetie," she said as she turned toward me. "I don't think Brian is up yet."

Fear built inside me. Who turned off the light then? I pivoted on my heel and headed down the hallway to his door. I quietly opened it and was met with Brian's soft snores. Hand shaking, I shut his door.

Could the boy in my dreams turn off the lights? Had he somehow made his way into my waking hours? I stumbled into my room and frantically shoved my bare feet into my tennis shoes. I pulled the black hair tie from my wrist and pulled my still-wet hair into a ponytail.

As I walked to the front door, I said, "Grandma, I'm going for a quick run."

I didn't hear her reply as I yanked the front door open, jumped the three porch steps, and took off running. I wanted to run until I collapsed. I needed to run until the fear coursing through my veins subsided.

My long, strong legs pushed me forward faster and faster. The fear lessened as the hot sun beat down on me. My muscles burned with exertion. Panting, I started to decrease my pace. Sweaty tendrils of hair clung to my forehead. My legs wobbled like jelly.

Was I imaging all of this? Were my dreams and the trick with the light switch some new symptom of my psychosis? Was I losing control of myself entirely? Fear surged through me again. I needed to talk to Rebecca. I turned and jogged toward her home.

Slowing to a walk, I trudged up her driveway and went into the garage, where I kicked off my shoes and knocked.

"Hey, kiddo," Rachel, Rebecca's mom, said as she opened the door.

"Hi, is Rebecca up?" I asked.

"Yeah, she's in her room," she said.

"Thanks," I said. My shoulders relaxed, and I took a deep breath. This house was my haven. I knocked softly on Rebecca's door.

"What?" she said.

I opened her door. "It's me."

"Oh, hey. I thought you were my mom." Rebecca sat up in her bed and put her phone down. She frowned as she studied my face. "Is everything okay?"

I sat down on the cream shag rug in the middle of her room and started to pick at stray strands. "I don't know. I'm freaking out. The mandated counseling makes me feel like something is seriously wrong with me. I'm scared."

Rebecca scooted off her bed and joined me on the rug. "I'm sorry, but hopefully counseling can help you learn to deal with your past," she said. She was the only one of my friends who truly knew about my psycho dad.

I nodded but rushed into my latest problem. "I'm having really bad dreams too. And this morning while I was in the shower, the lights went out. All by themselves. Brian didn't do it. The door was locked from the inside, and the power was on in the rest of the house. I checked the switch, and it was pushed into the off position."

"Oh my God!" Rebecca said, grabbing my shoulders. Her eyes were wide.

"I know, it practically gave me a heart attack," I said. Her hands slid off my shoulders and into her lap.

"Maybe there's something wrong with the light switch," she said, brows raised in hope but her voice full of doubt.

"Maybe. I'll ask Grandma to check it out," I said. It was a rational explanation, but I didn't believe it. "With Dad gone, I thought my life would get better, but it's still a mess."

"Come on, it's not. Your life is getting better. I think the counseling will help you," Rebecca said, nudging my knee with her hand.

I could feel her stare. Her need for me to be OK. My eyes met hers, and I tried to smile.

"Are we still on for the pool today?" she asked.

"Yeah," I said. I got up from the floor. "I'll go get my suit. Meet you there at noon?"

"Sounds good," she said. "Jess, you're fine. I promise you."

I nodded and shut her door quietly. Her assurance didn't work. My gut swirled in warning, but I ignored it. I could pretend everything was OK. I had been doing it for years.

CHAPTER 13

BRIAN

My car tires crunched over gravel as I pulled into the pool parking lot. I parked under a large red maple tree for shade. I didn't want to burn my ass off getting into a hot car after swimming. Our community pool and tennis courts were set between cornfields but sheltered by a thick growth of large, mature trees. The low hum of music spread into the parking lot. Sweat beaded on my forehead as I signed in at the front gate. Squinting, I scanned the grassy lawn for Jessie and Rebecca. I spotted them in the main area. Will was stretched out on a lounge chair next to Jessie. The urge to move him away from my sister was automatic. I shook it off. He was a good guy, and Jessie was growing up, as much as I hated it. I pulled a lounge chair from the dwindling stack and walked toward them.

"Hey, how's it going?" I put my chair next to Rebecca.

"Good." Rebecca smiled at me. "Is Tracey coming?"

"No, she has to work," I said. I looked to Jessie, expecting her hello. She barely waved at me and didn't make eye contact.

It was awkward between us. She was upset with me for telling Grandma about Mrs. Palmer, which landed our guidance counselor in Jessie's counseling session. Jessie was afraid of what Mrs. Palmer might say.

She turned to Will. "You want to get in?" she asked.

"Yeah, sure." He walked over to the pool with her, pausing beside a tile that put the depth at five feet.

I reached over and grabbed the lounge chair Rebecca was on and shook it a bit. "What's up?"

She took out her headphones. "A whole lotta nothing, which I'm enjoying," she said with a smile.

"Good deal." I wondered if Tim, my best friend, had been in touch with Rebecca. As much as he tried to downplay it, I knew he liked her. I didn't want to tip her off by bringing it up, so I planned to ask him later.

I put in my headphones. "Bad Decisions" by the Strokes played. Stretching, I leaned backed and tapped my foot to the beat. It was great to hang at the pool. I hadn't been here at all this summer. The sun soaked into my skin. My muscles relaxed, and my thoughts drifted.

Cold water splashed across my stomach and chest.

Gasping, I jerked forward to see Jessie dropping a cup in the grass and running back into the pool. I pulled out my headphones and ran after her. She was going to pay for this. I dove in after her.

She squealed and hid behind Will as I advanced on her. Will laughed and held his hands out in front of him. He moved backward in the water, Jessie clinging to his back.

"You can't protect her, dude," I said.

"I told her not to do it," Will said, laughing as he backed away from me.

Jessie peeked over Will's shoulder. "You deserved it."

I reached around Will and grabbed Jessie's arm. I quickly got both of my arms around her and squeezed.

"Say you're sorry," I said.

"Not happening," she said.

I plunged us both under the water. Jessie struggled in my arms like a hooked fish. What was I thinking? I moved my legs to the side to protect my boys. She wasn't above hitting me in the nuts. Lena certainly would.

Jessie stopped squirming and went still. Fear zipped up my back, and I immediately released her. What if Lena showed up?

I surfaced at the same time as Jessie. She quickly moved behind Will again.

"Are you done now? Can I relax in peace?" I said in mock annoyance.

I studied her face, searching for the hard lines characteristic of Lena. Looking for eyes that appeared older, different, and darker. Jessie stared back at me over Will's shoulder.

"I guess," she said and flipped me the bird.

Hand skidding across the water, I splashed them both. I waded to the edge of the pool, lifted myself out, and huffed back to my chair. She was such a pain in the ass sometimes.

As I lay back down, I could hear Will and Jessie laughing and splashing each other in the water. Good thing Will improved her mood.

"Feeling refreshed?" Rebecca asked.

"Yeah, smart-ass," I said. Rebecca chuckled as I shoved my headphones back into my ears and attempted to relax. Through my slitted eyes, I watched Jessie's familiar form come into view, Will following behind her. Grabbing their towels, they started drying off.

"Rebecca, Will has to go to work. Do you want to ride back to my house with us?" Jessie asked.

"Yeah, sure." Rebecca sat up and gathered her things. She nudged my foot. "See ya later."

"Later." I shaded my eyes with my hand and watched them leave.

Will's Jeep rumbled to life, quickly followed by the loud guitar riff of "Voodoo Child" by Jimi Hendrix.

Will had no idea how close he was to a voodoo child. For his sake, I hope he didn't piss her off.

CHAPTER 14

JESSIE

Rebecca and I started giggling as soon as we shut the front door behind us. Happiness radiated from me. Visions of a sun-drenched Will with the wind ruffling his golden hair played in my mind. I practically floated into the dining room.

"What are you girls giggling about?" Grandma asked from her seat at the dining room table. The ever-present smell of coffee filled the kitchen as we passed through. At the threshold to the dining room, I stopped short. The drawer to the china cabinet was open, and all of our family pictures were spread out on the table. My mom had stuffed family pictures in those drawers for as long as I could remember.

"Oh nothing," I said.

"I'm sure it has nothing to do with a certain cute boy who just dropped you off." Grandma winked at me.

My cheeks flushed with heat. To redirect her attention, I asked, "What are you doing with the pictures?"

"I thought we could make Mom a photo album and take it to her the next time we visit," she said. It had been three weeks since Mom's suicide attempt.

"Good idea," I said, grabbing a chair. Rebecca sat beside me and picked up one of my baby pictures.

"Seriously, you had the roundest head," she said.

"Yeah, I know," I said. We both cracked up.

Smiling, I rifled through the pictures, picking up shots of Brian and me. I avoided the ones of my parents. My whole body tensed, and my stomach rolled, when I spotted the pictures piled to my grandmother's right. All of them featured my dad. She must have been sorting them out of the album. I agreed. I hated seeing his face—especially his eyes—even in photographs.

"Who's this?" Rebecca said. She handed a me a faded high school graduation picture. The boy in the picture had a thick mop of dark hair and an awkward smile. Something about his eyes indicated he wasn't comfortable with himself.

I was certain I'd met him before, but I couldn't pinpoint where. Frowning, I handed the picture to Grandma. "Do you know who this is?"

Grandma took the picture and sighed. "It's your father's graduation photo," she said. Her wary eyes met mine. My mouth went dry. I took the picture from Grandma and studied it. It was the boy from my nightmares. I hadn't recognized him before—he had an abundance of dark hair, and I'd only known Dad as bald—but I couldn't mistake the resemblance or my gut reaction.

I dropped the picture and pushed back from the table. Baby, my ever-present shadow, followed me to my bedroom. I picked her up and curled my body around her on my bed. I stared at my cream wall, breathing in her musty, hay-like scent and trying to slow my pounding heart.

"Jessie, what's wrong?" Rebecca called from my bedroom doorway. I waved her into my room.

"Remember how I mentioned I was having awful nightmares?" I asked.

"Yeah," Rebecca said.

"There's a guy in them. You know, like our age. He's full of hate and rage. He tries to kill me in my dreams, to strangle me. The picture of my father? That's the guy."

Rebecca sat down on my bed and scooted right next me. Her closeness comforted me.

"That's completely freaky. Are you sure it's him," Rebecca asked as her lips disappeared into an anxious line.

"I'm sure," I said, staring forward at nothing. A mental break was coming. One more straw would do the trick.

"Maybe it's some weird subliminal thing. Like you'd seen a picture of him as a teen before, and your memory pulled it into your dreams. Like some weird therapy," she said with her brows raised in question.

I rubbed my forehead. "That's a really good theory. I'm impressed you came up with it."

We both laughed, which eased my fear a bit.

My reprieve didn't last long. Rebecca had to go home, and the photo of Dad kept flashing in my mind like a waking nightmare. Dad was still the problem, even now. Even from the grave, he was trying to kill me.

CHAPTER 15

BRIAN

Rain and wind hammered against my window. I rubbed the sleep out of my eyes and picked up my phone. The display read 3:33 a.m. The front door noisily creaked open and then quickly squeaked shut. *What the hell?*

I jumped out of bed and pulled on shorts and a T-shirt. I grabbed a baseball bat from my closet and quietly eased my door open. Peering into the hallway, I didn't see anyone. But Jessie's bedroom door was open, and upon further inspection, I found her bed empty.

I quickly straightened. *Shit.* What was she doing? I strode down the hall and slipped out the front door, hoping to catch up with her before she vanished into the night. I wasn't sure who was in charge: Jessie or Lena. Either way, a three o'clock trip outdoors in the pouring rain was never good.

A white streak caught my eye. She was running down the middle of the road in her white, knee-length nightgown. I stifled my urge to yell out to her and charged into the rain. If this was Jessie, she had completely lost her mind. She turned down the dead-end road toward the woods.

"No, no, no," I muttered to myself. I was fifty feet from her when she disappeared into the woods. "Jessie!" I yelled before I could stop myself. She didn't hear me over the gusting wind and rain.

I raced after her, the knuckle of a twisted tree root sending a shot of pain up my heel. Shit, my feet were bare. I slowed and placed my feet carefully on the muddy path. The sound of the storm was slightly muffled by the thick growth of trees. Wiping my eyes, I cautiously followed my sister.

My heart sank. She was going to the foxhole. My father's true resting place.

I could hear her talking as I approached. She fell to her knees next to the gaping hole and shouted, "I won't die for you! This is your fault! It's your fault you're dead! Yours!"

Her dark hair swung forward, covering her face. She grabbed handfuls of dirt and threw them into the hole. She fell forward on her hands, her body shaking with sobs.

It wasn't Lena. Lena didn't cry. I rushed toward her. She shrieked and scrambled backward.

More proof this was Jessie. Lena never appeared scared, and the girl in front of me wore fear on her face.

"It's me!" I said, reaching for her. "What are you doing?"

Wet hair clung to her pale face. Her wide eyes darted to me and then the hole. "I don't know," she said. Her shoulders slumped, and she hung her head.

I grabbed her elbow and helped her get up. "Come on, we have to get out of here."

She avoided my stare but meekly followed along. Meek was not her thing. It reeked of giving up, and she couldn't give up. I wouldn't let her. The rain pelted my skin the whole way home, but it washed the mud from my feet.

The front door creaked again as I opened it, and I cringed. I hoped Grandma wouldn't wake up.

"Stay here. I'll get a towel," I said. Jessie shivered and dripped on the entryway rug while I went into the laundry room. I threw a towel to her and wrapped the other around myself.

I motioned for her to follow me to the dark family room. We sat on the carpeted floor.

"Tell me what's going on with you," I said.

She sniffed and stared down at her hands. "Like I told you, I keep having nightmares about a guy trying to kill me, but now I know who it is. Yesterday, Grandma and I were looking through all the old pictures shoved in the china cabinet, and there was a high school graduation picture of Dad. The boy in my dreams is Dad. I didn't realize it until I saw the pictures yesterday," she said.

"I don't know. Maybe you saw that picture some other time, and it just stayed in the back of your mind," I said.

"This is why I didn't tell you. Who's going to believe me? I've never seen that picture of Dad. Not ever," she said.

"OK," I said, backing off. Jessie wasn't one to exaggerate or be dramatic. But this was too awful. After all we had been through, this couldn't be happening.

"It's real." She leaned toward me. "He's trying to kill me. He says it's my fault he's dead." She pressed her fingers to her eyes. "That's why I went to the foxhole tonight. To tell him it's not my fault."

"This is just too weird," I said.

"But it's happening!"

I extended my hands to her, palms up. "I believe you. It's just hard to wrap my head around. You're talking horror movie shit," I said.

For a moment she seemed lost in thought, but in the next instant she awoke with inspiration. She scooted closer to me. "Do you remember the palm reader from Alyssa's birthday party? The one who told me I had a dark twin?"

Our neighbor Ted had thrown his wife, Alyssa, a carnival-themed birthday party last year. I frowned at first, and then my brow relaxed as I remembered the lady with gray-streaked black hair posing as a palm reader. She had gripped Jessie's hand and insisted she listen to a grim warning.

"Yeah, I remember her. Why?"

"She knew about my twin just by reading my palm. Maybe she would know why Dad is haunting me. Or how to stop him," she said.

I had been angry at the woman for scaring Jessie. I remembered her pushing a card across the table and into my hand. Her dark-brown eyes had locked with mine. She'd said I would need to contact her.

A wave of surprise crashed over me, quickly followed by shock. I did have the card. I had stuffed it into my junk drawer at the top of my dresser.

Jessie watched me intently, waiting for me to speak.

"I have her card," I said quietly, still reeling from the implications. Events matching up and connecting themselves rang of destiny.

"You do?" Jessie raised her eyebrows hopefully.

"I'll call her, but you have to explain to her what's going on." I understood something was going on, but I wasn't the right person to recap it.

"Can we call her tomorrow?" she said.

"Let's wait until Grandma isn't home," I said.

Jessie nodded. "I'm going back to bed now. I'm freezing." She sniffed again and pulled the towel tighter around her shoulders.

"Yeah, me too," I said. I watched my sister head back to her room. I was glad she was calmer, but now I was the one who wanted to run away. Jessie didn't see how things were lining up.

I shook myself. No matter what happened, I wouldn't lose my sister.

CHAPTER 16

JESSIE

The uniform brick ranch houses of our neighborhood rolled by as I stared out the car window. I wasn't looking forward to seeing my mom today. I loved her, but my feelings for her were twisted with betrayal. It had been four weeks since her suicide attempt, and Brian had seen her a few times already.

Given my attack on her doctor, I hadn't been allowed to visit until I learned some calming techniques to get through tough situations. The counselors at the Oaks had told me to look around for five things I could see and to say them out loud. To pay attention to my body, think of four things I could feel, and say them out loud. *My feet are warm in my socks*, I thought as the car merged onto the highway. *I feel the cushioned seat beneath me.* It did seem to help.

Grandma reached over and patted my hand. I lifted my lips upward in an attempted smile. In many, ways I wished Grandma were my mom. I trusted her, and she had kept me safe when my mom hadn't. We pulled into the hospital parking lot. *The sidewalk is hard beneath my tennis shoes.*

I glumly trudged behind Grandma as we made our way to the behavioral health center. The woman giving out badges started in her seat when our eyes met. I quickly lowered my gaze. Great, she recognized me from the incident with Mom's psychiatrist. I was glad I didn't remember, but on the other hand, I would like to watch a video of it. What would a fearless, angry version of me look like?

The atrium had high ceilings with skylights that invited the afternoon sun. Light drenched the abundant surrounding plants, giving the space a bright, airy atmosphere. My mom sat alone at one of the tables, sipping a cup of tea. She wore a tan sweat suit, and her dirty blond hair was clean and styled. Grandma approached first; I hung back.

"Oh, Jessie. I'm so sorry." Mom's eyes welled with tears. She stretched her arms out to me, but I leaned backward avoiding her embrace. My anger flared and burned in my chest.

She dropped her arms to her sides and hung her head. Her thin frame trembled, and her face crumpled in pain. My anger receded just as quickly as it had come. Her pain became mine.

I reached my arms around her and pulled her to my chest. We were the same height now: five feet, seven inches tall. I couldn't bear to see her hurting. She clung to me like a life preserver. Several deep breaths later, she let go.

Wiping her cheeks, she sat down, and Grandma and I joined her at the table. She pushed a small, cherry-stained jewelry box toward me.

"I made you a little something to hold your earrings," she said, smiling hopefully at me.

The top had an indented square carved into it, which she'd filled with small gold and pink enameled hearts and covered with lacquer. It was pretty clear she had taken some time to arrange the hearts perfectly.

"Thank you. It's very pretty," I said, smiling back at her.

"That's beautiful, sweetheart," Grandma said to Mom while squeezing her hand.

"They give us craft materials to work with. It helps to keep your hands busy," Mom said.

I ran my finger over the little hearts on the jewelry box while we sat in awkward silence. Mom straightened her shoulders and sat up in her seat.

"I am sorry. I should have never tried to take my life. My thinking was so confused and muddled. I just wanted the pain to stop," Mom said.

Her eyes searched mine while her hands twisted nervously in her lap. The apology I really wanted was one for her failure to protect us, for her failure to acknowledge Dad's toxic behavior.

"OK. Is that all?" I asked, hoping against reason she'd take the chance to address the real issue in our relationship. Yes, I was upset she'd tried to take her life. But I was even more upset she'd decided to stay with him, no matter the pain he caused us.

"I don't know what else to say, Jessie, besides I'm sorry," she said, reaching outward, palms up.

My shoulders dropped. "Right."

Her eyes were clear, and she seemed present, but it wasn't the time to say how mad it made me. How tired I was of all the drama in my life. How my own sanity was now at stake because of my parents. I could say none of those things, at least not right now. I would continue to put my mom's fragile mental health first and forget about my looming psychosis. I hung my head and picked at my cuticles.

"We can talk more later," Mom said.

I nodded. Grandma jumped in to fill the silence. She showed Mom some samples of kitchen cabinet finishes, part of a home-rejuvenation project she'd talked Mom into doing before her suicide attempt. She had hoped it would get Mom engaged in life. But decorating was more Grandma's thing than Mom's.

Furtively, my gaze wandered around the room. Some of the patients had visitors, while others sat alone. A woman with gray, bobbed hair, who I guessed was in her late sixties, made eye contact. Her defeated gaze mirrored my own. Life was insurmountable at times, like a looming tidal wave poised to overtake me. I nodded at her. She rewarded me with crinkled eyes and a tentative smile. My heart ached for us all. Other people's pain was like my own at times.

I gave myself a mental shake. There was a lot of good in my life too: Grandma, Brian, Will, and Rebecca. I had to focus on them. This place was where you went to recover when life got the better of you. I would not give up.

CHAPTER 17

BRIAN

I put on my headphones, and "Under Pressure" by Queen flooded my brain as I waited for Jessie to get ready for her first counseling appointment. Wow, what an appropriate song. I rubbed my fist against my palm.

There were two conversations I didn't want to have today. Our future call to the palm reader and this one.

I shook my head. Shit, I was a coward. I had asked to attend Jessie's first session with her new counselor for dissociative identity disorder. What other choice did I have? If Jessie was going to get better, her counselor had to know what I had experienced with Lena. Well, *most* of it. I wanted to influence the narrative. Jessie was angry but not so violent that she was a danger to herself or others. Her biggest fear was being kept in some type of inpatient facility. And I shared it. I didn't trust anyone to keep her safe.

Grandma reluctantly agreed to Jessie and I going alone. She got it. We were in this together. She didn't know about Lena, and filling her in on that would have to wait. I walked down the hallway toward the front door. The fruity, floral smell of Jessie's shampoo permeated the bathroom and hallway. Removing my headphones, I popped them into their case and shoved them into my jeans pocket.

Warm summer air blew into the house as I opened our front door. A clear blue sky stretched for miles overhead. My black 2018 Malibu gleamed in the driveway. Two years ago, I had installed a Cherry Bomb muffler and loved the rumble. I wanted to sit in my car and chill with some music until Jessie was ready. I turned the ignition. "Alex" by Roy Blair erupted from the speakers. Bobbing my head, I mouthed the words to the lyrics.

"Good song," Jessie said as she slid into her seat. I nodded and put the car in reverse. The music was so loud it stopped any conversation. *Should I say anything before the session?* I hesitated to turn the music down. No need to get Jessie worked up before we even got there.

Twenty minutes later, I maneuvered my car into the parking garage. The day was already sweltering, and I didn't want to leave it exposed to the brutal sun. I pushed my hair back from my sweaty forehead and walked with Jessie to the lower level of the Oaks, where the counselors had offices.

"What's the office number again?" I asked.

Jessie dug in her shorts pocket and pulled out the card. "It's 111."

I noted the numbers next to the offices and paused in front of Dr. Chen's open doorway. She looked up from her computer and turned toward me with a smile.

"Hello, may I help you?" she asked.

"Yeah, I'm Brian Taylor, and this is my sister, Jessie." I tugged Jessie's arm until she stood beside me.

"Great, I'm Dr. Chen. I'm so happy to meet you both," she said. She rose from her chair and walked toward us. She wore white dress pants and a light-blue top. Her hazel eyes quickly studied Jessie and me. She waved her small hand toward a cream love seat and black, modern chairs. "Please have a seat."

Jessie walked over to the love seat, and I sat down beside her. Dr. Chen settled into the chair closest to us. Glancing around her office,

I noticed the pale-yellow walls and her framed degrees in psychology. A small rock garden rested on a coffee table in front of the love seat.

"Let me explain how I typically work with patients," Dr. Chen said, directing her gaze toward Jessie. "I am familiar with your history, as Mrs. Palmer reviewed it with me, but I would like to hear why you think you are here." She paused a moment. "Also, I understand Brian would like to provide some input during our initial discussions."

"OK." Jessie took a deep breath. "I think I'm here because my friends and Brian have told me about some out-of-character things I've done, but I don't remember them."

"I think it's very brave that you're willing to explore what's happened." Dr. Chen smiled encouragingly. "Do you have any idea why you don't remember?"

Jessie looked to me for assurance. I met her gaze and nodded.

"Maybe PTSD?" Jessie said, her eyebrows arching.

"Brian, what would you like to tell me?" Dr. Chen turned her body toward me.

I rubbed the back of my neck and exhaled. If therapy were going to work, we needed to tell Dr. Chen as much as we could. "I really don't want to say anything at all, but I need you to have all the information."

Jessie wrang her hands as she sat next to me. I wished for us both that we could avoid this.

"Bravery must run in the family," said Dr. Chen.

"I don't know about brave." I shook my head like a defeated bull. "Anyway, you probably know about Jessie attacking my mom's psychiatrist."

"Yes, I'm aware," Dr. Chen replied. Her hazel eyes watched me calmly but intently as I spoke.

"That wasn't the first time Jessie lost her temper," I said. "Lost her temper" was a wild understatement of Lena's rage.

Jessie jiggled her left leg. I looked over at her. Her pained expression made my heart sink.

"Brian, let me just interrupt a moment, as I can see this is upsetting for Jessie," Dr. Chen said. "Jessie, nothing that we discuss here leaves this room unless I have your permission to share it."

Jessie slumped forward in her seat and nodded.

"My sister told me Mrs. Palmer mentioned dissociative identity disorder to her. I googled what it meant, and she has those symptoms." I wiped my hands down the front of my jeans. "I mean, I've interacted with Jessie when she seemed to be someone else. Someone who's older, physically strong, and angry. This person told me her name was Lena."

In that instant, the room changed. All the hair on my arms rose.

Lena straightened in her seat and twitched her foot like an angry cat's tail. I was afraid to look at her.

CHAPTER 18

LENA

I blinked several times, allowing my eyes to come into focus. This room was not familiar to me. Brian sat on my left. The attentive female and pale-yellow office walls didn't convey any threat. There didn't appear to be any immediate danger.

"What are you doing?" I asked Brian.

He put his head in his hands. Color drained from the woman's porcelain complexion as I waited for Brian to respond. I raised my brows in question. "And you are?"

She cleared her throat. "I'm Dr. Chen, Jessie's counselor. And you?"

I smiled at her boldness. She didn't fear me. "I'm Lena."

She extended her hand to shake mine. I just glanced at it. "I don't touch people unless I want to."

"Fair enough," she said, allowing her hand to lower to her lap.

I pushed Brian's shoulder, noting his discomfort. "Snap out of it, pansy. I'm not going to hurt you."

He jerked his shoulder away and glared at me. "I know that."

"Why are we here?" I said. My foot twitched in agitation.

"Your little stunt with Mom's doctor landed us here. You've made your presence known," Brian snapped.

I shrugged. "Incompetent old man had it coming."

Brian quickly stood. "Excuse us for a minute, Dr. Chen."

"Oh." She paused for a moment, clearly surprised. "All right."

He motioned for me to follow him out of the room. This could be fun. Brian walked a little way down the hall. He turned to face me and put his fingers to his lips.

"Understand that if you talk about your violent tendencies in front of Dr. Chen, she may think Jessie is a danger to herself and others. My sister is afraid of being committed to some facility," he whispered.

"Why did you bring my name up then?" I sneered.

"I'm trying to help Jessie. And I didn't think you would show up in this situation," he said.

He pushed his hair off his forehead. The bitter stink of fear rolled off his body.

"Jessie was afraid. She needed me," I said.

"What makes you show up?" Brian asked.

"If she's significantly distressed, angry, or scared, I come to deal with it." I enjoyed talking about myself and might've kept going if a more pressing thought hadn't occurred to me. "What if the doctor asks about Dad's death?"

Smiling, I remembered the run to the woods. The thrill of Dad chasing me like a stupid beast. The joy of seeing his crumpled body at the bottom of the foxhole. Best night ever.

"What are you smiling about?" Brian asked, indignant.

"Nothing," I said, widening my eyes to feign innocence.

"Don't say anything about Dad's death. Pretend you weren't involved. If the therapist thinks you're a danger to other people, she will have you committed. I don't want Jessie drugged to the gills and held in some facility," he hissed.

"Agreed. What if she asks me other questions? Jessie may pull me into future sessions," I said.

"Just don't talk about your desire to hurt certain people." Brian's gaze met mine and then darted quickly away.

"Yeesh. It's not that many people. Like one—or, well, two." I rolled my eyes.

"This is serious." Brian's eyes locked to mine.

Sensing his desperation, I said, "No problem." I obviously scared him, but why? Hadn't I already proven I would protect him as well?

"Good," he said with a nod. "We have to go back."

He turned and walked back down the hall. I moseyed along behind him, already bored.

We reentered Dr. Chen's office. I flopped down onto the couch next to Brian and laid my arm across the back of the love seat.

"Is everything OK?" Dr. Chen asked.

"Yeah, we're fine," Brian said, cringing away from my arm.

Dr. Chen met my stare. "Lena, correct?"

"Yes," I said.

"Thank you for speaking to me today. I want you to know you and Jessie are safe here."

I studied her face. I could easily read other people, their intentions and motivations. I didn't sense a threat. "I'm not concerned with our safety," I said.

She nodded, her hazel eyes never leaving mine. "I would like to speak to you in the future. Would you be willing?"

I glanced at Brian. He apparently had no input, as he blankly stared into space. With his hunched shoulders, he appeared to be close to losing it.

I shrugged. "Sure, I don't mind. Just ask for me by name."

"Thank you. I appreciate it." The corners of her mouth flicked upward. "May I ask for Jessie to come back now? I need to talk to her about how therapy can help her, and I'd like to ease any concerns she may have."

"I don't need to be around for the logistics chat anyway," I said, leaning back into the couch cushions and closing my eyes.

CHAPTER 19

JESSIE

I clawed my way out of a deep, dark hole and into consciousness. My body was heavy with fatigue. Brian's insistent voice demanded my attention.

"Jess, wake up." He prodded my shoulder. I wiped my mouth with my hand and struggled to sit up.

I realized where I was and jerked into complete awareness. Panic zipped through my body.

"What happened?" I asked, reflexively leaning toward Brian. I had lost time again. Pain pulsed incessantly through my head.

"Jessie, everything is fine. You're safe here," Dr. Chen said. She extended a small paper cup of water to me.

I took it from her and downed the water in two gulps. Fingers tapping my parted lips, I wondered why she was telling me I was safe.

"OK…" I said slowly, afraid of what had happened while I was out.

"Good. I just wanted to make that clear." She pointed to my wrist, where I wore a bracelet with a silver wheel. "Your jewelry is very pretty."

"Thank you. Brian made it for me," I said, glancing at my brother. He stared blankly ahead.

"I'm impressed." She smiled at Brian. "It looks like a dharma chakra, a wheel of truth."

Brian smiled mechanically, but I raised my brows in question.

"It's a symbol of enlightenment in Hinduism and Buddhism."

I nodded. I had noticed the praying Buddha statue on her bookshelf.

My hand closed around the symbol on my wrist. The wheel was warm from my body heat. I always wore my good luck charm.

She handed me two sheets of paper. It was a survey titled "How Much Do You Dissociate?"

The word *dissociate* sent a shiver of fear down my spine. I had read articles about it, but it was still a lot to understand. I nervously adjusted my position on the cream couch.

"I would like you to answer the survey so we can discuss it during your next appointment," she said. "Also, here is my card. I write a blog about dealing with dysfunctional family, based on my own experiences. Check it out, as it will help you understand my background and how I may be able to help you."

I took the card from her. "Can we stop for today? My head is killing me," I said, grimacing.

"Of course. We've done a lot of good groundwork today. Regarding the survey: Don't be nervous about filling it out. Everyone dissociates to some degree to deal with stressful situations."

"They do?" I piped up in surprise.

"Yes. Hopefully that makes you feel a little more comfortable," she said.

"It helps," I said, nodding in agreement.

"If you have any questions, please feel free to give me a call," she said. Brian and I shared a look .We'd call, but not with just any question. Some issues were better left to a psychic.

By the way she watched my interaction with Brian, I assumed she was gauging my support system.

"Will do. Thank you," I said. Brian and I rose from the couch and made our exit.

We walked to Brian's car and settled in. I held Dr. Chen's card and survey in my sweaty hands. I looked over at Brian. "We still need to call the palm reader about my bad dreams," I said.

Brian forcefully exhaled. "We'll do it tomorrow. I'm at my limit for sharing today."

His face was creased with worry. And I was tired.

"Yeah, me too." I leaned further back in the seat, wishing I could hide from my life. We drove in silence toward home. I stared out the car window but only noticed the gray-and-white blur of downtown Stanton followed by miles of green cornstalks now at their full height.

We pulled into our driveway. The glass pane beside our front door framed Baby's excited face. I loved her happy little tail and wiggly hind end. I opened the door, scooped her up, and rubbed her silky ears. She tried to lick my face but could only reach under my chin. "Yes, I love you too my li'l sweetie," I cooed.

I walked into the kitchen and put Baby down. A Mariano's pizza box sat on our new cream-and-gray-speckled countertop.

"Did you order me pizza?" I asked fervently hopeful. My mouth was already watering. Brian pushed past me and sat at the counter.

Grandma turned to me with a smile. "Of course. I thought you might be hungry after your appointment," she said.

I set Dr. Chen's card and survey on the table and lifted the lid of the pizza box. The rich, spicy smell of pepperoni and melted cheese escaped. I sat down on a bar stool and dug in. Brian followed suit.

As I chewed, Grandma studied Dr. Chen's business card and then picked up the survey. The furrow between her brows deepened. Her hand crept up her body and slowly covered her mouth.

Her eyes rose and met mine. I swallowed.

"Do you have these symptoms?" she asked, her voice trembling. "You feel separate from your body? You lose track of time?" She sucked in a gulp of air. "People tell you you've done things you don't remember?"

I reached out my hand for the paper, and she gave it to me. Brian stilled beside me.

My eyes skimmed the directions. I had to rate how often I experienced certain events on a scale of one, which meant "never," to ten, which meant "very often." I knew after a quick scan I had a handful of tens.

"Yeah, I have some of these," I said quietly.

Grandma moved around the counter and sat down heavily at the dining room table.

"I'm partly to blame for what you're going through. I should have said something years and years ago." She put her head in her hands.

I scooted off the bar stool and wrapped my arms around her shoulders. "It's not your fault."

"I'll have to work hard to agree with you." She smiled at me ruefully.

"I'll be fine. You'll see," I said, lifting the corners of my mouth in a small smile.

Brian and I locked eyes. I wanted them both to feel better. I especially wanted to feel better myself. I sent a prayer heavenward, asking for God to help me.

CHAPTER 20

JESSIE

I sat on our gray couch in front of the bay windows and watched for Grandma's car. Mom was coming home from the wellness center today. It had been six weeks since she tried to kill herself. My left leg jiggled incessantly. Why was I nervous?

Grandma had suggested I stay home versus picking Mom up with her and Brian. I obviously scared the crap out of the doctor. Usually I had a lot of empathy for other people if I thought they were embarrassed or feeling bad in some way, but regarding the incident with Mom's psychiatrist, I was numb. Maybe this was another point for me to check off on the dissociation survey.

A silver Volvo slid into the driveway. Baby jumped down off the couch and ran to the front door. I sat and watched for a few moments. I wanted to see the expressions on my mom's and Brian's faces unobserved. That would give me the real story, not the falsely positive talk I was about to hear.

Brian opened the back door of the car and got out. He squinted into the sun and extended his hand to steady Grandma. I smiled at my brother. I loved his manners.

I didn't notice or pick up on any tension. He moved and spoke with ease. Grandma's face, which sometimes screamed "I'm gonna lose my mind," was relaxed as well.

Always the drunk's kid, I never stopped analyzing people and situations. Would that ever change? I bet not. I rose to open the front door.

"Hi, honey." Mom pulled me into an embrace. "I missed you."

It may have been the natural thing to say, but it didn't feel genuine. She only missed Dad. "I missed you too," I said while absentmindedly patting her back. I hadn't missed her either, not really. I met Brian's gaze as he waited behind Mom. He raised his eyebrows up and quizzically lifted one side of his mouth.

The jury was out. Mom appeared OK, but I never knew what shoe would drop next. I walked with Mom into the dining room, and she sat down. Brian took her bags back to her room. Grandma had zoomed into the kitchen to make some coffee. I watched my mom's face as she settled in. Her eyes were bright, alert, and clear. Before, she had been exhausted, with bloodshot eyes and a zoned-out stare.

She scanned the kitchen and took in the new cream cabinets and the trendy black, white, and gray countertops. I couldn't help my smile. I loved the silky smoothness of the cabinets.

"I've missed your coffee," Mom said as she lowered her steaming cup. She smiled at Grandma and took a deep breath. "It's like coming home to a new house with all these updates."

"Don't they look great?" Grandma said.

"Yes, they do." Mom sighed. She met my gaze. "Your dad and I had picked out the old ones."

She obviously still cared, but I sure didn't.

I had hoped she would be pleased with the updates. We desperately needed a fresh start.

CHAPTER 21

JESSIE

I smoothed my hair down while critiquing it in front of the entry-way mirror. Will was coming to pick me up soon. My heart raced with the thought. Yeah! It was time for normal life stuff, time to forget about my troubles. I cringed; it sounded a little pathetic even in my own head.

I heard the purr of his Jeep moments later. I opened the front door and gave him a bright smile and a wave. Movement from the passenger seat had me jogging toward the car with curiosity. Oh my God! It was the cutest Irish setter I had ever seen. Its silky, dark-red coat gleamed. I could see its happy wiggles from where I stood, flabbergasted, in front of the car.

Will got out of his Jeep and walked toward me. His eyes sparkled with affection, and his warm smile drew me to him like a magnet. I stared in awe at his toned, tanned muscles. His straight blond hair blew to the side in the breeze.

"You brought your dog!" I practically yelled. When excited, I tended to be loud.

He laughed and said, "I know. Do you want to meet him?"

"Of course!"

He whistled and said, "Dakota, come here boy."

The dog jumped through the open window and bounded over to us. I knelt so he could smell me. He had beautiful tawny eyes. I was in love. I turned my head and laughed as he licked my face aggressively.

"Dakota, sit," Will said. The dog complied but wagged his tail furiously.

I smiled. "He's gorgeous!"

"Thanks." He smiled back at me. "I thought we could take him for a walk through the forest preserve."

"Yeah, I would love that," I said. The forest preserve had great walking and biking trails. It was nothing like the mostly wild woods at the end of our street.

I rubbed Dakota's head as Will walked me to my side of the Jeep. He opened the passenger door, and Dakota bounded into the back seat. What a smart dog. I was impressed. We hadn't taught Baby anything other than potty training.

All loaded up, we headed to the forest preserve. As we neared it, I could see the tall, green and gold ornamental grasses swaying with the breeze. The field stretched for miles before us. Large, old oak trees provided the only landmarks in the sea of grass, though I could make out a graveled walking path. It was a mild, blue-sky kind of day, which was unusual for August, but I was thrilled with the break from the heat.

Will reached for my hand as we started on the path. Dakota had obviously been well trained as he walked sedately along Will's left side. He didn't move ahead of him or lag behind. Baby was so small that if we took her for a walk, she panted after one mile.

I relaxed my hand in Will's, comforted by this small connection. It was so different to be with him versus my ex. Alex had mainly wanted to go somewhere private to make out, but Will wanted to talk and get to know me. The sting of Alex's betrayal and my yearning for him had faded considerably. I liked Will for more than his kisses. I valued his friendship too. It was good to just be around him. I couldn't tone down my wide smile.

He must have been reading my mind because he bent down and planted a soft kiss on my lips. We stood still on the lightly graveled path, our foreheads touching.

"More, please," I said, and an irresistible smile broke across Will's face.

"Happy to." We kissed and kissed some more. The heat of his lips against mine mesmerized me. The charged space between us shrunk as we pressed closer together. My body hummed with the electricity between us.

The jerk of Dakota's leash brought Will back to earth. He pulled away, and I sucked in a ragged breath. Dakota dug his claws into the gravel and pulled Will toward the field. He momentarily had the advantage with Will off-balance. I glimpsed a rabbit darting deeper into the grass.

"Dakota, no!" Will said and righted himself. Dakota stopped pulling but whined in clear distress. "Rabbits make him crazy. He loves to chase them."

"I see that," I said. A string of saliva hung from Dakota's mouth.

Will motioned to a bench under a tree farther ahead on the path. "Do you want to sit down for a few minutes?"

The sound of his voice was muffled by the pounding heartbeat in my ears. I wondered if he was as shaken by our kiss. "Sure," I said.

My legs shook as our fingers laced together. The sun had started its descent, filling the sky with pink and orange. The path had grown quiet as we walked deeper into the preserve.

We settled on the wooden bench with our sides pressed together.

"What's the oldest song you have your phone?" Will asked.

I furrowed my brow in concentration. I picked up my phone and started to scroll through my music.

"I don't know if it's the oldest, but it's pretty old. It's by Etta James: "I'd Rather Go Blind.""

"Nice. Play it." Will reached for my phone and hit the play button. Etta's smooth voice floated outward.

We sat comfortably without speaking, nodding our heads to the song.

"You've got some soul," Will said after the last notes hung in the air.

"What have you got?" I said, grinning. I tapped his phone.

He scrolled through his music library and then showed me his screen. "How about this one?" he said.

The song was "My Immortal" by Evanescence. Pain and power poured out of the phone. As someone who loved to sing, I could imagine the singer filling her lungs with air and pushing out incredible sound and emotion. For me, it wasn't just singing; it was feeling and expressing in its purest form.

"She's amazing. I like your pick better than mine." We sat there smiling and gazing adoringly at each other.

"I know, right? She has an incredible voice," he said. "Just like someone else I know." He lightly touched my nose with his finger.

I gave him a quick kiss for the compliment.

"How're you doing with your mom back home?" Will asked.

I lifted one side of my mouth in an attempted smile. He always wanted to know if I was all right. I loved him for it.

"She seems better, more stable," I said, shrugging. "I'm still mad at her for trying to take her own life. We have a long way to go before I feel OK around her."

"I can't imagine," he said, squeezing my hand.

Dakota rose from the ground near our feet and shook out his coat.

"I think that means he's ready to go." I didn't want to talk a whole lot about Mom.

Will watched Dakota affectionately. "Yeah, I guess so. We probably should leave before it gets dark."

Only a shimmer of fiery orange remained on the horizon. The idea of being out here in the dark did not appeal to me. If I had been with Brian, I would have been safer. Not that there was any danger nearby, but experience had taught me anybody could be a weirdo, and Brian gave off I'm an alpha-male, don't-mess-with-me vibe. Will's vibe was easygoing.

We picked up our pace and headed back to the Jeep. The parking lot was empty. Will opened my door, and Dakota jumped into the back seat. I put my arms around Will's waist and hugged him. He smelled fresh and clean, like a dryer sheet. He wrapped his arms around my shoulders and squeezed back.

Our bodies were pressed together from thigh to chest. A little shifting landed my arms around his neck and his around my waist. He pulled me even tighter against him. Our lips meshed perfectly, as if we had been kissing forever. Damn, he was good.

Will's hand slid into the hair at the back of my neck, and chills rose all over my body. When we finally broke apart, it was fully dark.

"Wow," he said. His warm, sweet breath washed over my face.

"I know." Desire flooded me, but I said, "We should go." I jumped into my seat before we could kiss again. If we started, I wouldn't want to stop.

Our entwined fingers rested on his thigh as we drove back to my house. Dakota quietly lay across the back seat. My whole body was relaxed, which was such a rare state for me. We pulled up in front of my house moments later.

Brian's car was gone, but someone was home. I could see the TV's flickering blue light through the bay windows. I wanted to invite him in, but it was too soon. I didn't know how Mom would react.

Will kept the car running, so I thought he understood my hesitation. "Thanks for tonight," I said.

"Yeah, it's always good to see you," he said as he squeezed my hand. "Sucks that school is starting up again soon."

That comment came out of nowhere.

"Yeah, it is." My lips pursed.

"I was thinking we should make it official. You know, you and me as a couple," he said, smiling hopefully while his eyes searched mine. He seemed confident of my answer but not overly so.

Warm pleasure filled my body. I would love to call him my boyfriend. In fact, I would be proud to call him my boyfriend.

"I'd like that a lot actually," I said, my smile spreading from ear to ear.

He pulled me into an embrace, and we kissed again. Movement in the bay window caught my eye. My mom peered out at the driveway.

"I better go. My mom," I said as I motioned toward the window.

"Yeah OK. Text me later," he said.

I climbed out of the car and practically floated up the driveway to the front door. A wide smile stretched across my face. Happiness must make you buoyant. Before I went inside, I waved at my new boyfriend.

CHAPTER 22

BRIAN

As I pulled into our driveway, I stuffed the last bite of my ketchup-drenched cheeseburger into my mouth. Ketchup slid down my finger and plopped onto my jeans.

"Shit," I said, groping with my free hand for the napkin on the passenger seat. I wiped my hands and scrubbed at the ketchup on my jeans. Wadding up the trash from my midnight snack, I walked into the garage. I threw the fast-food bag in the trash can and entered the house through the kitchen. The place was quiet, with the lights off in the kitchen and living room. I walked down the hallway toward my bedroom. Grandma and Mom were obviously in bed for the night, as their doors were closed. Light seeped from under Jessie's door. I knocked lightly.

"It's me." I rested my hand on the handle, poised to enter.

"Come in," Jessie said.

I found her sitting up in bed with a book open on her lap. Baby wagged her tail at me from the foot of the bed. "What's up?"

"Not much." She moved her legs to the side of the bed to make room for me.

"How was Mom today?" I had spent the day with Tracey's family. We'd celebrated her mom's birthday. But I couldn't go to sleep without checking on my own mom. I also wanted to see how Jessie was doing. With her reading a book, she appeared relaxed.

She raised one side of her mouth in a grimace and shrugged.

"She seems better. More alert at least," she said.

"Good," I said.

Grandma had been sleeping in my room since she moved in with us, so I slept on the couch in the family room. I stored my pillow and blankets in Jessie's room.

I bent down and picked them up. "I'm going to crash."

Just as I was straightening, slow, heavy footfalls thumped from the direction of the kitchen. It was a sound I had not heard since Dad died. A sound I had dreaded even then. It meant he was home.

I dropped my blankets.

Jessie gasped and sat up straight. She placed her hand on Baby's back to silence her. She knew the sound and what it meant as well as I did.

"What was that?" she whispered.

I peered down the hallway. Mom and Grandma were asleep. Their bedroom doors hadn't opened. The footsteps softened, as if they'd reached the carpet. Which meant one thing: They were headed down the hallway toward the bedrooms. Toward us.

No, no, no, my brain screamed. Frantically, I searched Jessie's room for something I could use as a weapon. I badly wanted the baseball bat that was in my closet.

"Get in the corner," I whispered. She scrambled behind me with Baby in her arms and pressed herself against the wall. I grabbed the curling iron off Jessie's dresser. Squaring my feet and facing the partially opened door, I listened as the footsteps steadily approached.

My pounding heartbeat provided the only background noise.

At Jessie's doorway, the footsteps stopped. Except for a square of light filtering from the room, the hallway was dark and empty. I didn't see anyone. Jessie emitted a low moan behind me.

Nothing happened for a few long seconds, but then I detected hazy movement. A column of dusty air rotated for a minute and then zoomed back down the hallway toward the front door.

I huffed out a breath, gathered my courage, and charged into the hallway, smashing my lips together so I wouldn't scream.

The hallway was empty. Panting, I sprinted toward the front room with Jessie close on my heels. The front door was closed. I turned toward the kitchen. The door to the garage was closed as well. I jogged into the family room only to see the sliding glass doors firmly shut.

"What in the hell?" I cried. The dusty column had disappeared.

Jessie held Baby to her chest as she scanned the kitchen and family room.

"I don't know, but I'm seriously freaked out," she whispered. She paced around the room, jerking like a puppet on a string.

"I did see something," I said.

"What?" She gasped. "Did it look like a tall, thin boy?"

I moved back to the front of the house and checked the driveway and yard from the living room window. Jessie followed closely behind. Nothing appeared to be wrong. There were no cars driving by. The only movement was from the large silver maple trees blowing slightly in the breeze.

"No, it looked like a dusty column of rotating air. Kind of like what you'd see in a dust storm," I said, brushing sweat-slicked hair from my forehead.

Frowning, Jessie said, "That's a new one."

"Yeah, seriously." We stared wide eyed at each other.

My pounding heart started to slow. There wasn't an immediate danger, it seemed. But what the hell had just happened? Wrapping my head around it wasn't possible.

Something dawned on me. Lena hadn't shown up, and Jessie had been very scared. I frowned, studying Jessie's face. It was her. The hard lines of Lena's face were not apparent. This meant something; I just didn't know what.

We stood in the living room like statues, listening for the slightest sound and trying to detect even the smallest movement. The sweat dried on my skin, and I started to chill. I shook my head to clear it.

"I don't know what that was, but let's go sit in the family room and watch TV or something." I didn't need to explain away the sound of the footsteps. We both knew what they were. It wasn't some random noise the floorboards made. It had been my father's footsteps walking down the hallway.

"OK," Jessie said, her shoulders slumping in relief. "I'm going to get my blanket." She headed toward her room.

I eased onto the couch, grabbed the remote, and turned on the TV. My body felt like broken glass. The tension was taking its toll.

Jessie came into the family room with her blanket draped around her shoulders and Baby close on her heels. She sat down at the other end of the couch.

"Hey," I said. Her head swiveled toward me. "I'll call the palm reader tomorrow."

She nodded in agreement but said nothing.

CHAPTER 23

JESSIE

Baby licked my face with abandon. I got my hands up to hold off her love attack. I struggled to sit up and noticed Brian asleep at the other end of the couch. I rolled my stiff neck side to side. The fragrant smell of hazelnut coffee drifted into the family room. I held Baby to my chest and shuffled into the kitchen.

"Hey, sweetie. You guys fall asleep on the couch last night?" Grandma asked.

"Yeah," I said.

The fear from the night before was nowhere to be found in our sun-soaked kitchen. The buttery smell of biscuits and coffee permeated everything.

"The biscuits smell great," I said, putting Baby down and rounding the counter to get a cup of coffee. Grandma would let me have one cup, but that was it. She held her arms out to me. I easily walked into them and stooped down to rest my head on her shoulder. When had I gotten taller than her? She rubbed and patted my back as she always had.

"I love you, sweetie," she said, kissing the side of my head.

"I love you too," I said. It was nice to have her love and attention. I had a sense of safety with her, which was something I never had with my own mother. I lifted the corners of my mouth in a tired smile and retrieved my favorite black mug, with a gold design of "Don't Mess with Me" printed in bold letters on the front. My stomach rumbled in anticipation of hot biscuits with butter and red raspberry jam.

"Grandma?" Brian called from the family room.

"Yes," Grandma replied.

"Can you make some bacon too? I'm so hungry," he said.

I rolled my eyes. I was pretty sure he told Grandma every morning he was very hungry.

"Of course, honey," Grandma said.

What didn't she cook for him? Brian moseyed into the kitchen with Baby dancing around his feet for attention. He stooped down and absently patted her head. Grandma poured him some coffee and slid it across the counter to him. Seriously, he was so spoiled.

"Do you have plans today?" Grandma asked.

"Yeah, Jessie and I are going to go get some stuff for my dorm room," Brian said.

"Oh, good. That will be fun," Grandma said. She turned back to the fridge and reached for the bacon.

I wasn't aware of any shopping plans. I shot a questioning look at Brian, but he shook his head quickly while Grandma wasn't looking. A lift of my chin indicated I got the message. We were going to see the psychic.

After we finished breakfast, I followed Brian to his room. He flicked on his light. I stood in the doorway while he sorted through the mulch of forgotten pens, paper, and trinkets in his top dresser drawer.

"Got it," he said, holding up the slightly battered white card. I stepped into his room and took the card from him. It read "Natalia Moretti, Psychic Medium" with her email, phone number, and address.

I met Brian's gaze. "You'll call her?" I said, holding my breath hopefully. I had absolutely zero clue on how to start that conversation.

"Yeah," Brian exhaled and pushed his hair off his forehead. "Go get ready so we can go. I'll call her from the car," he said, his lips pressed together in a grim line.

My stomach cramped in anxious anticipation. I hurried to the bathroom to get ready.

Once we were both ready, we headed out. Ten minutes later, we pulled into the Target parking lot. Brian turned off the car radio and plucked his phone out of the cup holder.

"OK, here we go," he said. He dialed the number and pressed the speaker button.

I could barely breathe. A female voice answered the call.

"Hi, Natalia?" he said. "This is Brian Taylor. We met not quite a year ago at a friend's birthday party. You gave my sister, Jessie, a reading."

I heard her responses as Brian paused to listen.

"My sister and I wanted to know if you could talk to us about a ghost. I mean, it seems like a ghost," Brian said. He rubbed his forehead in clear distress. "Um, how much is it for a session? OK, we can do that. Today? Yeah, we can at meet at one in the afternoon." His eyes darted over to my shocked expression.

She confirmed her address and provided driving directions. I couldn't wait to hear what she had to say. I hoped she could give us some information. But my entire body prickled with anxiety. I wanted to know but was scared to hear the truth.

Tears spilled down my cheeks. I couldn't stop the overflow of emotion. I was deeply scared about what was to come.

"Jess, we can do this. We'll figure this out," he said.

I vigorously wiped the wetness from my face. "Yeah," I replied.

"We've got about twenty minutes to buy school supplies, and then we need to drive to her office." Brian got out of the car and strode toward the Target entrance. I had to jog to catch up with him.

CHAPTER 24

JESSIE

The heavy plastic bag full of school supplies cut into my palm. I was amazed by what we had managed to buy in twenty-five minutes. We settled our purchases in the back seat of Brian's car and headed toward downtown Stanton. The houses situated on the outskirts of town had been turned into a variety of offices for insurance providers, tax prep companies, and other locally owned small businesses.

Natalia's office was in a charming two-story home with forest green siding and black trim. The adjoining buildings were similar, except the siding of one was dark blue and the other a smoky gray.

Their normal, professional appearance brought me some measure of relief. I had imagined a big sign featuring mystical-looking palm art and offering readings.

I exhaled and straightened my shoulders in preparation for this very unusual conversation. We entered via the wide front door. Brian read her card and said she was in office number two. What would have been the formal living room and dining room were now enclosed and made into offices. The sign on her door read "Inspired Guidance Counseling, Natalia Moretti." Brian knocked lightly.

She answered with a subdued smile. She was slightly shorter than I was, with thick salt-and-pepper hair coiled into a bun at the back of her neck. Her welcoming dark-brown eyes appraised us.

She motioned us to a Southwest-styled couch and sat next to us in a matching chair. I scanned her office as I settled in. It was open and sunny, with several thriving potted plants. The fresh smell of mint tickled my nose.

"I'm Brian Taylor, and this is my sister, Jessie," Brian said, motioning toward me with his thumb.

"Yes, I remember you from the party at the steak house," she said as she stared into my eyes. "Thank you for coming. I thought I would see you again. I believe certain souls are meant to cross paths, even briefly."

Wow, we were jumping right into it. I was surprised as the truth of her words resonated through me. I leaned toward her.

"The last time we met, you said I had a dark twin," I blurted. The need to know more about my twin blocked my fear.

"Yes, I can feel the shadow of her presence here. She's always listening," Natalia said.

"How do you know that?" Brian interjected.

"I hear and feel messages from spirits. You may be familiar with guardian angels." Her questioning gaze studied us. Frowning at each other, we shrugged.

"Yeah, we know about guardian angels from church, but not a lot," I said.

"My guardian angels give me messages for other people. Specifically when people ask and give permission for me to receive answers on their behalf."

She gave a slight smile. With her hands folded neatly in her lap, she was the picture of tranquility.

The idea of guardian angels wasn't too unbelievable; I prayed to God for help all the time. I didn't know how all the God stuff worked, but I did sense a presence. I had God-given gifts that helped me endure this life: Brian, Rebecca, my intuition, and the ability to run fast.

Her explanation made sense to me. "Um, OK. I give you permission to ask questions on my behalf," I said.

"Thank you," she said with a nod.

Brian piped up. "We called you today because we think there might be a ghost in our house, and we don't know what to do."

"I understand. Wait a moment." She held up one finger and then slowly let it drop back into her lap. She leaned back against the chair, took a deep breath, and closed her eyes.

Bewildered, Brian and I quickly glanced at each other and then back to her. A minute passed. She took another deep breath and opened her eyes again.

"Your father has refused to move on after his passing. He has chosen to wander the earth," she said.

Shocked, my eyes nearly bulged out of my head. I believed her, but the confirmation blew my mind.

"Do you mean he's the ghost in our house?" I sputtered.

"I mean—"

"Wait a minute," I shouted incredulously before she could answer. "Is he allowed to do that?"

She chuckled quietly. "All humans have free will. We are born with the right to choose our path."

"I mean, if you're dead," I said, spreading my hands wide, "shouldn't somebody come and take you somewhere?"

Brian leaned toward her with his mouth hanging slightly open in a stunned stupor. His eyes were glued to Natalia.

"Your guardian angels do come for you when you leave this life, but you can refuse to follow them," she said.

"Did you know our dad was dead before we got here?" Brian said, narrowing his eyes. "As a police officer, he was mentioned in the *Stanton News* when he died."

"I didn't know your names until today. I don't know your father's name, but my guides are telling me your father is the lingering spirit in your house," Natalia said.

Her eyes unfocused as her gaze turned inward. She lifted her hand, her palm facing us. "His spirit is showing up in his adolescent form?" she asked.

Her eyes locked onto mine, and I nodded in shocked silence.

"Showing up as an adolescent speaks to his emotional maturity. His spirit is impulsive, angry, and irrational. He's learned to invade your dreams, and now he can manipulate things in the physical," she said.

I stared at her in horror, my stomach churning. I leaned against Brian for support.

"How do we make him go away?" I whispered. "Can your angels ask him to go away?" I prayed for an easy solution. Fear and worry welded me in place.

Her face sobered, and she appeared older than before. "I'm sorry. I can't. It's something you must resolve with your father. If a hardship is part of your life path, if it's something you signed up to learn before entering this life, your guardian angels will not prevent the lesson. I know it's a difficult concept to understand."

She reached her hand out for mine, and I let her take it. Her warmth enveloped my cold fingers. "Your father's anger is focused on you. You must stand up to him and take your power back. Owning your power is something many struggle with, but for you it will be critical."

I jerked backward in my seat, pulling my hand from hers. "How am I supposed to do that with a ghost?" My mind spun with how very wrong this could go for me. I flung my hands upward in exasperation. "Do you not understand he wants to kill me?"

In the next instant, my worst fear crystalized. "*Can* he kill me?"

"If his spirit has learned to manipulate energy and move things in the physical, he can cause you harm," she said, her eyes never leaving my face.

Brian, who had been mostly quiet, erupted. "No! That can't be." He stood and swayed slightly. All color had drained from his face, and his eyes were wild. His desperation startled me.

"Brian," I pleaded, "sit down." I grabbed his arm to pull him into his seat.

Natalia's eyebrows rose in question, but she didn't otherwise acknowledge Brian's outburst.

"I know it's hard to believe, but I won't sugarcoat it. My guides show me you've fought him off before in a dream by surrounding yourself with white light," she said.

Again, shock rumbled around my dumbfounded body. She was exactly right, and no one knew the details of my dream except me.

Brian used my silence as an opportunity to jump in again. "What about her dark twin? She's shown up and defended Jessie in the past. Won't she come and help with this?"

Natalia's brows furrowed for a moment and then released. "No, Jessie's twin can't help in this situation. Her twin is a physical being. She's absorbed a lot of the rage Jessie feels. She can only affect physical things, not spirits. But Jessie can. It's her soul, the essence of who she is, that must stand up to your father."

I absorbed Natalia's words and then looked to Brian for his reaction.

He hung his head and muttered, "That's why she didn't show up last night. There's nothing she can do." He snorted. "I was hoping she would be able to help." He ruefully glanced at me and then dropped his gaze.

Natalia scooted to the edge of her chair. "Your guardian angels want you to find your own power to fight off your father. You have shouldered his aggression since you were very little. You are strong. Feel the love and strength in your heart and grow that energy."

I rocked back and forth on the couch. The possibilities over-whelmed me. "I can't do this," I said as I twisted my bracelet around my wrist repeatedly. "I don't feel strong physically or emotionally."

I remembered my dream. White light had come from my heart, and when I focused on it, it grew stronger. But it had been so hard to accomplish. It had been mentally exhausting.

"The problem is, I couldn't hold the white light. I could protect myself briefly, but I couldn't sustain it."

Brian let out a long exhale. A brief glance at his creased face let me know how worried he was.

"Jessie, try this: First, do some breathing exercises. Put your hand on your heart, take a deep breath in, hold it for a second, and then let it out slowly. Do this three times," she said.

My hand moved to my heart, and I took a deep breath in, held it, and slowly released. It did calm me.

"Now visualize the white light and surround yourself with it. Ask your guardian angels to guide and protect you as well. Make the white light as bright and dense as possible. Practice this over and over until you can conjure the light at will. When you've achieved it, demand your father come to you."

Breaking my concentration, I exclaimed, "I'm not calling for his ghost! No way."

"You must," she said insistently. "You have to call him, as it gives you the upper hand. He is responding to your command, and it sets the battleground as yours."

She studied my face closely. "Do the breathing exercises and visu-alize the white light every day until you are confident of your ability. Only summon him then."

"I understand," I said. On one hand, I deeply understood that what she was saying was true. I would have to battle my father's ghost to find peace. But on the other hand, how could this be happening? I didn't want to accept it.

"I have something to protect you until you've accepted your own power and mastered the white light," she said. She rose from her seat and went over to her desk. She pulled open the top drawer and removed a black velvet pouch. She stretched open the drawstring bag and shook something into her palm.

"This is a black tourmaline pendant. It will help create a shield of psychic protection around your aura and deflect negative entities. It should protect you against your father's energy."

Natalia dropped it into my outstretched hand. A hexagonal black tourmaline hung from a long black string. I slipped the necklace over my head, and the smooth pendant settled between my breasts under my T-shirt.

"I know this is a heavy burden, but you've already been through the worst of it. This is the way to put your father to rest," she said. "If you have questions or need to talk, please call me."

"Wait!" I flung out my hand. "What about my dark twin? Why do you call her that?" I asked, desperate to know more.

"I call her a dark twin because she is filled with rage. It's a powerful emotion. In time, she could greatly influence who you are."

"Do you mean she could take over and be present all the time?" I said scared to hear the answer. Brian and I stared at each other with bated breath.

"I don't think that will happen, but at some point, to release the rage, you will need to forgive your father for what he's done," she said.

That would be a cold day in hell.

"The important thing is, you don't want her to take over, and your intent is critical," she said.

She was holding something back; I was sure of it. But before I could ask anything else, she glanced at her watch and said, "I'm sorry. I need to wrap up our session. I have another client."

"OK. Thank you," I said quietly. I had so many more questions.

Brian stood and reached into his pocket for the sixty dollars we owed her.

I stumbled out of her office and into the bright summer day. Brian followed me to his car, started it, and cranked up the air conditioning. Hot air blew on my face.

He turned to me. "I don't know what to think about that whole meeting," he said. His bewildered gaze searched mine. "Do we need to find a Catholic priest for an exorcism or something?"

I burst out laughing. Brian joined me seconds later. My stomach clenched with each new outburst.

Leave it to Brian to lighten the mood. I wiped my eyes. "Honestly, what she said is true. In my dream, he did look like a teenager, which is why I didn't realize it was him until I saw his high school picture."

Brian rubbed his right palm against his left fist. "I don't know how to help you," he said with fear stamped across his face.

"You do help me. You're here," I said, meeting his gaze. "I'll do what she suggested."

I didn't know any other way to handle it.

CHAPTER 25

JESSIE

The August heat and humidity clung to me during my morning run. I slowed my pace and settled into a cooldown. Anger and frustration seeped from my pores along with the sweat. Running had helped me release the emotions I had bottled up in my body.

Mom would attend a counseling session with me today. I continued to be angry with her for not protecting me, for not behaving like a mother should. Dr. Chen insisted I address this with my mother and try to let go of the anger. Based on what Natalia had said, forgiveness was important.

Still, my mom's made-up reality, in which Dad had loved us, drove me crazy. I couldn't understand her behavior or what drove it. I wiped my sweaty forehead with my shirtsleeve and pushed my tired body toward home.

A few hours later, Mom and I sat in Dr. Chen's pale-yellow office. Mom's gaze wandered around the room, her hands fluttering nervously in her lap. She sat in the chair next to the love seat, so Dr. Chen rolled her desk chair across from me.

"Thank you for coming," Dr. Chen said, smiling at Mom. "I realize this can be nerve-racking, and I appreciate your courage."

Nice, Dr. Chen. I nodded in admiration. She understood my mom perfectly. It *was* brave for Mom to attend counseling. My mom loved me, but she didn't want to believe my issues were caused by her or Dad. News flash! My issues had a direct correlation to them both. I wanted to shout, "Welcome to the party! Jump on in. The water is freezing and dangerous."

Mom leaned toward Dr. Chen. "Thank you. I want to help Jessie in whatever way I can."

Her eyes crinkled at the corners as she smiled at me. Her obvious affection made my anger subside, with some compassion squeezing into its place. Why was I emotionally stronger? Mom's affection was childlike. She loved us, but she couldn't seem to put our needs ahead of her own.

"I think it would be good to start with what brought us here today," Dr. Chen said. "As you know, Jessie attacked your doctor in the hospital after your suicide attempt."

Mom blinked rapidly, obviously taken aback by the doctor's directness. Dr. Chen paused a moment and then continued. "Jessie and I have spoken about it, but I think it would be good if she shared her feelings with you."

Mom leaned back in the chair and stared at her lap. "OK," she said quietly, not meeting my stare.

I waited for her to look up, but she didn't. I shifted my gaze to Dr. Chen, hoping for direction. She nodded and motioned with her hand for me to continue.

I twisted toward my mom, addressing the side of her face. "I just remember your doctor coming out of your room that morning and he said, '*You survived.*'"

Mom's brows furrowed, and she glanced at me.

"Initially, I thought it was an odd thing to say, but then it made me furious," I said, grimly recalling the scene: the sterile hospital hallway, the old doctor, my shock at his words. "I don't remember anything after that."

Brian, of course, had filled me in on what had happened. The echo of Lena's anger swirled around my body. In case she was listening, I mentally gave her firm instructions to stay away.

"Why would he say that?" Mom said, genuinely curious.

I dropped my head back against the couch and stared up at the ceiling in disbelief.

"Because it's been hard to survive," I said, jerking my head down. "Your doctor acknowledged it had been hard for us to survive! I don't understand why you didn't see it. Why didn't you kick him out of the house? I begged you to, but you never did."

My body strained toward her. Tears welled in my eyes and dropped onto my hands. I drew a shaky breath and let it out slowly, vainly trying to reign in my overwhelming sorrow.

"I'm sorry," Mom said, her face crumpled in anguish. "I was trying my best to hold our family together."

Dr. Chen grabbed tissues from her desk and pressed a few into Mom's hand and the remainder into mine.

"I would do anything to protect you," Mom said quietly.

"But you didn't! Why do you think we're sitting here?" I said, throwing my hands into the air.

Dr. Chen reached toward me in a calming gesture. "Jessie, do you mind if I interject here?"

"No, that's fine," I said, struggling to find my own composure.

"Thank you," Dr. Chen said. "It may seem like your mom had the ability to leave your father, but I bet she was trapped as well."

Mom's stare met mine, and I saw all the pain in my eyes echoed in hers. Mom left her seat and knelt in front of me. Her arms encircled me for a hug. The mountain of anger I harbored shrank as she cradled me.

After a moment, Mom sat back in the chair and wiped her face. "I did feel trapped. I kept hoping he would get better. He was seeing a therapist for his drinking," Mom said, her eyes imploring, hoping for some understanding.

As she spoke, I understood my mother was as much a victim of my father's abuse as we were. She didn't know how to deal with him.

"In domestic abuse situations, women commonly feel trapped," Dr. Chen said. Mom flinched at the term *domestic abuse*.

As Dr. Chen continued to speak, a better understanding dawned within my heart. Mom had done the best she could for us. I would just need to work on accepting her. The long journey to healing loomed large, like a vast, barren desert.

CHAPTER 26

BRIAN

I took a sip from the now warm can of beer and grimaced at the taste. Beer didn't appeal to me and the urge to keep drinking was absent, thank God. Being an alcoholic's kid, I was aware of the risks. I could spot problem drinkers right away: people who didn't want to stop once they started and people who became mean assholes while drinking. The happy drunks didn't bother me.

I scanned the going away party, looking for a trash bag. Tim's vast backyard was lit by white twinkle lights, which someone had strung in the trees, and a firepit. Folding chairs and high schoolers littered the yard. This was it. The last big party before we all left for college. My chest tightened painfully at the thought.

My eyes wandered to Jessie and Will, who sat near the firepit. She peered over Will's shoulder and frowned. I followed her gaze to see that Alex, her ex-boyfriend, had arrived at the party. Every muscle in my body tensed. Why would he come here? You'd think the guy would take a hint. This was not his crowd.

I found a trash bag by the back door and shoved my half-full beer into it. Tracey approached and slipped her hand into mine with a squeeze.

"What ya thinking about?" she said. "You look pissed."

I nodded toward Alex. "I can't believe he's stupid enough to show at this party."

Tracey's stare immediately focused on Jessie. I followed her gaze. My sister was intently watching the fire. She sat on the edge of her seat, and her face had hardened. The light had gone out in her eyes. Lena had taken over.

"No," I muttered and started walking toward her. Panic lit my body. Tracey pulled on my hand.

"Brian, stop. Maybe she won't do anything," she said, her face pleading.

Tracey knew about Lena, but she wouldn't recognize the immediate danger. I did.

Lena met my stare and lifted one side of her mouth in a slow smile.

"I'm just going to keep an eye on Jessie. That's it," I said. "She may cause trouble."

"Yeah, maybe," Tracey agreed, biting her lower lip.

We grabbed some seats farther back from the pit and across from Jessie. Our classmates stood in tight little groups as music blared from the speakers on the back porch. Tracey waved for her friends to join us, and they rushed over.

Jessie had kicked Alex in the balls last year. The savages at the party were probably hoping for a rematch. I ground my fist into my palm. Tension permeated the air.

Lena slowly rose from her chair and seductively snuggled on Will's lap. The two of them, heads pressed together, whispered to each other and then rose. Anger flared in my gut as they walked hand in hand, disappearing into the darkness.

"Shit," I hissed. This development didn't thrill me either. I gripped the sides of the chair and debated going after her. Lena might want to do things that Jessie wasn't ready for. The urge to chase her down was strong.

I watched for Alex's reaction. He glared at their retreating forms. Rebecca and Tim wandered over to us. Tim crouched down by my chair, while Rebecca stood with her arms crossed over her chest.

"You want me to throw him out?" he asked.

"No, he probably just wants the attention or an excuse to start a fight," I said.

"Yeah, what a douchebag," Tim said. He dragged two folding chairs over, one for him and the other for Rebecca. Alex stood with his best friend, Topher. Alli, Jessie's friend and Topher's girlfriend, was talking to them. She wouldn't want any trouble. Maybe she would talk them into leaving. Tim handed me a cold beer, and I took a few sips.

Ariana Grande and Justin Bieber's song, "Stuck with U," came on, and all hell broke loose. High-pitched girl shrieks filled the air as every girl at the party ran to one another and started singing and dancing. I shook the ringing deafness from my ears. Tim and I looked at each other in bewilderment. I shrugged and motioned for us to find our girls in the melee.

The song had broken the tension, and I couldn't fight my wide smile. Tracey and Rebecca, their arms draped over each other's shoulders, were singing. If Tracey was smiling, so was I. My hand landed on her shoulder, and my lips brushed her ear. "Can I cut in?"

"Absolutely," she said. She released Rebecca and wrapped her arms around my neck. We swayed to the music. I was going to miss this, the contentment of being with her. She was home to me. I pulled her closer.

I noticed Lena and Will at the edge of the group, slow dancing as well. A little relief eased my shoulders. At least I could see them, and nothing was happening. More partygoers joined the crowd, and I lost sight of her.

Things seemed cool for now. I closed my eyes and touched my forehead to Tracey's.

The music changed, and "Therefore I Am" by Billie Eilish boomed into the backyard. Girl squeals and lip-synching ensued. "I'm not your friend or anything / Damn" pulsed from the large speakers. Kids started pushing into me, forming a circle around Will and Lena. Lena lip-synched the words while staring directly at Alex.

"You think that you're the man," she sang while shaking her head and wagging her finger. A ripple of laughter ran through the crowd. She spun and faced Will, seductively swaying her hips from side to side. I closed my eyes. I didn't want to watch my sister's demon twin dance.

"You bitch," someone shouted, and my eyes snapped open. Gasps followed as kids hurriedly backed away. Without thinking, I shoved through the crowd. Will stood with his arms hanging loosely at his sides and his mouth hanging open. I followed his gaze to the grass-covered ground. Lena had Alex pinned, and her hand gripped his throat. I dove beside her, my tennis shoes digging into the dirt, and tried to pull back the steel-like grip she had on his neck.

"Come at me again," she hissed in his face, "and you'll end up dead." Alex's eyes widened with shock and fear.

Will unfroze and reached under Lena's arms to pull her away. At the same time, I was able to tug her hand away. It was a two-person job to get her off him. Lena's strength never failed to amaze me. Dealing with her was like living in a parallel universe. Things weren't quite as they should be; some vital piece was unfamiliar and altered.

Will and I each took an arm and hustled Lena away from the crowd. The sound of Alex's coughs behind me confirmed his survival. Once we were far enough away that no one could hear us, I turned to her.

"What in the hell are you doing?" I thundered.

Lena just peered at me with her dark, soulless eyes.

Will, looking distraught, hung his head and muttered, "She was belittling him for the crowd."

Lena, completely oblivious to the hurt in Will's voice, smiled at him.

"I'm not impressed," I said, glaring at her. "The party is over. You're coming home with me now."

With a hand on her hip, she snapped, "No, I'm not. Will is taking me home."

I locked eyes with Will, put my hands on my hips, and gave a quick shake of my head. Lena was leaving with me, no exceptions.

Will stepped closer to Lena. "I think it would be best if you went home with your brother," he said quietly.

"No. This is bullshit," Lena said.

Will's eyes widened in shock, and he stepped back from her.

I grabbed her upper arm and hauled her further away. "I will pick you up and carry you to the car. Do you want to embarrass Jessie this way? We both know you can't stay at this party," I whispered.

"Fine. You suck, by the way." Lena jerked her arm out of my grasp. She sauntered over to Will and kissed him on the lips. Will stood with his arms lax beside him. She didn't notice his lack of response.

"Let's go, party pooper," she said over her shoulder as she walked back toward the house.

I quickly sidled up to her. "You know, you ruined my night too. I was having a good time. But oh no. I have to babysit my sister's homicidal twin," I hissed.

"Boo-hoo," she said, giving me the side-eye.

We emerged from the darkness into the glow of twinkle light–covered trees. Tim, Rebecca, and Tracey rushed toward us, but I held my hand up to caution them. "It's OK, but we need to leave. Where's Alex?"

"He and Topher left. I'm pretty sure Alex was embarrassed," Tim said as he high-fived Lena. Her answering grin said it all: She was pleased.

"Not helping, Tim," I said.

"Right." Tim nodded and pretended to be subdued.

"Let's go." I motioned to Lena. Tracey, frowning deeply, fell into step with us on the way to the car.

"I'm sorry. You can stay if you want," I said, reaching my hand out to Tracey.

"No, I'll go with you," she said.

I squeezed her hand, grateful for her support. I was proud of my brave girl for sticking by me.

Lena didn't speak as she settled into the back seat.

Tracey walked around to the passenger side and got into the car. Her brows pinched together, and she turned in her seat to glare at Lena. "Why did you do that? Humiliating him like that makes you look really bad."

"Exactly," I added.

Lena shrugged. "Lighten up. He deserved it. Didn't he humiliate me at some party?" she said skillfully.

Tracey jerked forward in her seat. "Not cool," she said, crossing her arms over her chest. I squeezed her thigh and shook my head. I didn't want her to engage with Lena.

A cold chill crept up my back, and I shuddered. I had hoped that Jessie's counseling would stop Lena from showing up. I started the car and turned up the radio.

My body burned with anxiety. Lena was a complete psycho. Who would babysit her when I was gone? Maybe I should wait a year before I left for college. I prayed no one else had heard her threaten to kill Alex.

CHAPTER 27

JESSIE

We sat in the soft grass by the Stanton Riverwalk as the muddy green water swiftly flowed by. I pulled my knees to my chest and peered over at Brian. This was how we used to sit in front of the TV as kids. It was a comfort for us to sit together at night. I knew I was safer in his presence.

Just behind us, Mom and Grandma sat on a bench among the sun-drenched ornamental trees and flower beds. We were waiting for a table at our favorite breakfast place. It was across the street from the park, close enough that our pager would still work. I closed my eyes and tilted my face toward the sun. After breakfast, we were moving Brian into his dorm at Miami University for his freshman year. The city of Oxford was about forty-five minutes away, not too far but far enough. My heart ached with the thought of him leaving. My biggest supporter, my protector, would be gone.

The sounds of the babbling river, chattering people, and barking dogs enveloped us. Kids nearby were blowing bubbles toward the river. The glistening orbs danced over the water for a few moments before finally popping. Brian balled his right fist and pressed it into his left palm again and again. His hair was slightly oily in the front, as he had repeatedly pushed his hair off his forehead.

"We need to talk about what happened last night," he said.

I had gotten an earful this morning. I was deeply ashamed once I learned the embarrassing details. Alex wasn't completely innocent, but he hadn't deserved that display.

I took a deep breath. "OK," I said. "But it's not like I can control it. I want to. I *need* to, but Dr. Chen warned me that progress would take time."

She had officially diagnosed me with dissociative identity disorder.

"What scares me the most about last night…" He paused, taking a deep breath. "Lena was baiting Alex on purpose. She was trying to get a reaction out of him."

Chills erupted along my arms, and my stomach sank. Baiting Alex was not something I wanted to do. And it was obviously dangerous for him. Lena was out for revenge. "That's awful," I muttered under my breath.

"I know," he said. "You've got to talk to Dr. Chen about how to stop Lena from showing up. It needs to be your focus."

I fell back onto the grass and laid my arm over my eyes.

"I know it sucks, but you're in this situation, so you'll need to deal with it," Brian said.

"Along with fighting off Dad's ghost. No problem," I grumbled. I had practiced surrounding myself with white light, but it continued to be mentally exhausting. I still couldn't maintain it.

"Thanks for the pep talk," I said.

He nudged my leg. "Come on, sit up."

Grudgingly, I pushed myself up from the grass and sighed.

"I'm not going to be around to save you or anyone else from Lena's wrath. Ask Dr. Chen what you need to do to control her or something," he said.

"I will," I said with a little more conviction. Brian locked eyes with me and then nodded. I didn't know what he saw in my gaze, but he seemed satisfied.

The pressure of everything I needed to do weighed me down like an anchor pulling me into the watery depths. I dreaded Brian's absence. He had been my refuge for as long as I could remember. My one consolation was Grandma, but not even she knew me as well as Brian did.

He rubbed his face with his hands and groaned. "Man, how long is this gonna take? I'm starving."

"Yeah." I shrugged. "It's Sunday brunch. What did you expect?" I pulled the pager out of my pocket and checked for a notification. My stomach cramped with uncomfortable emptiness; I could relate to his impatience.

Mom and Grandma approached us on the grass. "Has the pager gone off?" Mom said.

I shielded my eyes with my hand as I peered up at them. Mom's eyes were clear and bright blue. The muddled confusion had gone. Her continued therapy was making a difference. She had a tan, healthy glow I hadn't noticed before. "Not yet," I said.

Mom checked her watch. "It's been an hour." She frowned and glanced toward the restaurant.

The pager buzzed. "Finally!" I said, showing them the blinking red lights.

"Nice." Brian jumped up and corralled Mom and Grandma across the street to the restaurant. He held the door open for them and said, "Ladies first." Grandma smiled indulgently at him.

I handed over our pager, and the hostess wove her way through the crowded dining area toward a table. The restaurant had bare brick walls, which amplified the sound of dishes clattering and people chatting.

Our server arrived—a college student, based on the sorority ribbon holding back her hair. She smiled directly at Brian.

"Hello. My name is Emma, and I'll be your server. What can I get you to drink?"

I fought the urge to roll my eyes. Brian attracted the ladies wherever we went. He smiled politely at her.

"I'll have a Coke," I said.

"Two Cokes," Brian said. Mom and Grandma ordered coffee.

"I'll be right back with that," she assured us, smiling hopefully at Brian.

"Are you excited to move in today?" Mom asked. She leaned toward Brian and placed her hand on his. Her increased engagement with us was something I was still getting used to.

"Yeah, excited and a little nervous," he replied.

"It's a big change, so that's completely normal," Mom said, patting his hand.

"I know you'll do well," Grandma said, beaming adoringly at him.

The waitress appeared with our drinks and glasses of water. "Are you ready to order?"

"Yes, I'll have your breakfast burrito," Mom said and motioned to me with her hand. "Jessie?"

"I'll have an order of pancakes with bacon and a side of your crispy diced potatoes," I said. The restaurant served the most delicious pancakes I had ever eaten. All the food was good. I could practically taste my buttery, syrup-drenched breakfast.

Brian ordered something called the ultimate skillet. I was confident it would be a huge pile of food. My eyes wandered around the restaurant as we waited. I wondered how Tracey was doing with her move to college. It sucked that her move-in date was this weekend; if it'd been next weekend, she would be with us right now.

Thankfully, our food arrived just fifteen minutes later. The only sounds at our table were the metal clanks of utensils scraping plates. I smacked Brian's hand away from my food when he tried to take a piece of my bacon.

"If you chewed your food, you would still be eating right now," I said around a mouthful of pancake. I swirled my last bite in the remaining butter and syrup. I leaned against the back of my chair and allowed my full belly to settle.

Brian sat back in his seat and stretched his long, muscular arms behind his back. "I think I'm going to have a nice nap on the drive to school," he said.

My brows furrowed with the thought of falling asleep in the car. Since our accident last year, I wasn't comfortable enough to sleep in a car. And now here I was, on a mini road trip with all the people who were in the wreck.

The collision had been the catalyst for the enormous changes in our lives. It was why Dad had fallen off the sobriety wagon, and it led to that fateful chase through the woods. In hindsight, it had been worth it. We no longer had to bear the oppressive presence of Dad in our home. I liked to think that since Mom didn't have the guts to make him leave, God had stepped in and removed him for me. I was eternally grateful.

CHAPTER 28

BRIAN

Finding the school wasn't difficult, as I had been there once before to tour the grounds. The University sprouted out of the farmlands and spread over an expanse of hilltop. A large wooden sign, painted cream and outlined in forest green, welcomed us to Oxford, the home of Miami University. Stately multistory red brick buildings with towering white columns greeted us. The grounds of the campus were beautiful, with meticulously maintained green grass, mature trees, and blooming flower beds. The outdoor space gave me a sense of peace.

I glanced at Jessie while Mom navigated to my dorm. She was sitting up in her seat, taking in everything around her.

"What do you think?" I asked.

"It's nice. Very pretty," she said, beaming at me.

Mom pulled into the queue of cars for the North Quad and Brandon Hall, my home for the next year. I was impressed with how organized the move-in process appeared to be. We had arrived at our allotted time and sat in the car until it was our turn to transfer all my stuff from the trunk to the big rolling bins awaiting us. Student helpers in matching T-shirts—red, with a white "Miami" proudly stamped across the chest—scurried from car to car, providing instruction and direction.

My stomach dropped as our turn approached. This was it; I would officially be on my own. I swallowed and opened the car door. Mom had already popped the trunk. A tall, thin boy approached me with one hand clutching his clipboard and the other extending for a shake.

"Hey, I'm Kevin, your resident advisor."

I gave his hand one strong shake. His handshake was firm as well. "I'm Brian Taylor. My dorm room is 216," I said.

Kevin reviewed the sheet of paper on his clipboard, found my name, and checked it off. "Yep, that's correct." He smiled. "Just load your belongings into the bins provided and head to the elevators, which are right through those doors. If you have any questions, you can come back to me or any of the RAs wearing these shirts," he said while tapping the letters on his chest. I nodded, and he hurried to the car behind us.

I grabbed one of the gray canvas bins and rolled it over to the trunk, which was full of boxes and luggage waiting to be unpacked in my new home. Jessie's eyes were bright with curiosity as she watched the move-in process unfold. I hoped she could see herself doing this someday.

We loaded all my stuff into one bin and queued up in front of the elevator while Mom and Grandma went to park the car. The line wasn't too long—only seven students ahead of me. A few of the girls in front of us had two overflowing bins apiece. How would it all fit in their rooms? Endless chatter filled the lobby as we maneuvered the bins into the elevator and pushed them to our rooms. The atmosphere added to my nervous excitement. A few of my high school classmates were attending Miami, but I had decided not to room with them. I thought it better to start with someone I didn't know so I could make more friends.

The elevator dinged at the second floor, and I pushed my bin into the hallway. The cart moved easily over the dark-blue, nubby carpet. The door to room 216 was wide open, but it didn't appear my roommate, Troy, had arrived yet. We had chatted a few times when we found out we were sharing a room.

Cool. I could pick which bed I wanted. I chose the one closest to the window, mainly for the fresh air. I didn't want to smell some dude's stink. It was a preemptive move on my part.

All the dorm rooms were off-white with dark hardwood floors. Unless it was a single, each room had two bedframes in a sturdy dark wood, with matching desks and dressers.

"It's nicer than I thought it would be," Jessie said, placing her hands on her hips as she surveyed the room.

"Yeah, I think so too," I said, both nervous and excited to be on my own. I'd struggled with the decision to come, but I prayed Jessie would be OK. It was selfish, but I couldn't put my life on hold.

I noticed the mini fridge and rolled it by the outlet so I could plug it in. Jessie grabbed the grocery bag on top of the bin and started putting the mini bottles of water into the fridge.

Grandma and Mom walked into the room, smiling at the sight of Jessie and I unpacking. "Oh, this is lovely," Grandma said.

"Jessie just said the same thing." I smiled back at her, but she didn't notice. She was pulling out drawers and inspecting them.

"Good thing you didn't bring a lot of clothes. It doesn't appear you have enough room for them. We'll have to rotate them throughout the year," she said. I could envision the mental list of tasks coming together in her head.

Mom handed the bedsheets to me and motioned for me to help her make my bed. We snapped them over the mattress, releasing their freshly laundered smell. Like my room at home, I had chosen light-blue sheets and a dark-blue comforter.

With three helpers, it didn't take me long to unpack all my belongings. I sat on my bed and pushed my hair off my forehead. Jessie stood by my dresser with a forlorn look in her eyes. It hurt to see her that way.

Guilt pinched my chest, and I couldn't meet her eyes. My gaze fell on the black string of her pendant, which was visible around her neck.

She continued to wear it day and night, but because the smooth, black, hexagon-shaped pendant had its own presence and would cause notice if she wore it openly, she always tucked it beneath her shirt.

Mom and Grandma looked around the room and realized there was nothing left to unpack. The time to say goodbye had come. It wasn't forever by any means. I was only forty-five minutes from home. I wanted to keep the mood as light as possible—for my sake and theirs.

"I guess that's it," I said.

"Do you want to go to the store and get any snacks before we go?" Mom asked.

"No, that's OK. I think I will walk around campus and map out my classes," I said.

"All right." Mom sighed. She walked over and wrapped her arms around me. "I will miss you so much," she said. As she pulled back, tears rolled down her cheeks.

Grandma hugged me next and let me know how proud she was. I fought the tight pain in my chest with a deep breath. Grandma put her arm around Mom's shoulders.

"Jessie, we'll meet you by the elevator," she said as she ushered Mom out of the room. She knew how close we were and how hard this separation would be for both of us.

Jessie lifted one side of her mouth in a grimace. She nervously shifted her weight from one foot to the other. She was trying to hold herself together. Hugging would open the emotional floodgates. Her eyes were tearing up already.

"I'll see you soon," she said, her voice breaking.

I nodded. "Keep wearing the pendant," I said, pointing to her chest. "It will protect you." With me away from home, the pendant would be her only protection. It felt incredibly wrong to leave her so alone.

"OK," she said softly. Chin trembling, she turned to go.

I watched her walk out my door as pain gripped my chest even tighter than before. It would be hard to give up my watch, my job as a big brother.

Who was I kidding? I would do as much as I could from here and go home when necessary. I pressed the heel of my hand to my heart, hoping to ease the pain.

CHAPTER 29

JESSIE

I stood in a dimly lit hallway lined with rich mahogany doors, three on each side of the hall. No, I was hypnotized and sitting on the couch in Dr. Chen's office. My awareness in this visualized scene surprised me. Maybe hypnosis was a doorway into a world where thoughts and reality met.

The door furthest from me on the right-hand side of the hallway opened, and a girl stepped out. I startled at the sight of my mirror image. Her lanky, toned form walked with a confident grace toward me. Vertical lines were etched on each side of her mouth. She was me, but older and tougher. Her gaze was ancient.

Fear simmered within me. "Lena?"

"Yes, I'm Lena," she said, her lips stretching upward in a warm smile.

Shock vibrated through me. If there were ever a time when I thought I might lose my mind, this was it. My hand shook badly as I slowly reached out to her.

She grasped my hand in hers and squeezed. "You're fine, Jessie. I'm just an older and much more aggressive version of you. But I'm still you," Lena said as she stared intently into my eyes. "We survived because of me. You have nothing to fear from me," she said smoothly and with confidence.

Stunned, I could only stare at her. Maturity and self-possession radiated from her. How did she know exactly what I needed to hear? Apparently, our feelings were linked. As I held her hand, I regained a piece of myself.

"Thank you for saving us," I said because she had, without question, protected me. And not just me. She had also saved Brian and Mom.

She acknowledged my gratitude with a nod.

"I'll do whatever is necessary to keep you safe," she said in a firm tone.

Brian's insistent command came back to me. I had to stop Lena's attacks.

"I am grateful for what you've done, but I think I'm safe now. I don't want you to attack anyone else," I said.

Lena's brows pinched together as she stared at me. It was otherworldly to maintain eye contact with another version of myself.

"Don't you think people should be punished for hurting you?" She paused a moment and searched my face. "I do."

"No." I shook my head quickly. I squeezed her hand. As gently as I could, I said, "You lured Dad to his death to protect me. And it was the right thing to do. He would have killed me. But I don't want to hurt other people. It's not necessary, and it's not the kind of person I want to be. It will cause more trouble."

"I understand," she said, her lips pressed into a grim line. Her displeasure was evident.

"Will you agree to not attack anyone else?" I asked firmly. It was essential to get her agreement.

She puckered her lips. "I will only attack someone if they are an immediate danger to your safety," she said.

I couldn't let her verbally wiggle her way out of this.

I squared my shoulders. "You baited Alex into lunging at me. I don't want you to do that. I only want you to respond if someone is a serious physical threat to my person."

She shifted her weight to her other leg and sighed. "Fine."

"Thank you." I let go of her hand and exhaled.

"Do you mind answering some questions for Dr. Chen?" I said. She shook her head. I moved aside so she could proceed to the part of my mind where my hypnosis began.

I quickly turned back to her. "Can we talk again sometime? There are so many questions I have for you."

"Yes, but you would need to be hypnotized, as you are now. Our two consciousnesses can only communicate in this space," she said.

I shook my head in wonder. She held my gaze for a moment and then turned to walk down the dimly lit hallway. After a few steps, she faded from view completely. I took a deep breath and let it out slowly. I studied the hallway. There were six doors, and Lena had emerged from one of them. Brian had mentioned a little girl, but I hoped to God I didn't have five more personalities to meet. As I started to back away, the door closest to me opened.

A little girl stood there, smiling shyly up at me. She wore a red checkered dress with a white tulle slip peeking out from the hem. I recognized her immediately. Her brown eyes sparkled with curiosity. Her smile displayed evenly spaced baby teeth and chubby, dimpled cheeks. My legs folded onto the hardwood floor in front of her. Love mixed with sadness overwhelmed me. This was my four-year-old self. My mom had a picture of me in this exact dress. It was one of her favorites.

Tears spilled down my cheeks as I smiled at her. "Hello," I said.

"Hello," she echoed. Her large, trusting eyes studied my face. She clutched a much-loved brown teddy bear to her chest.

"What's your name?" I asked.

"Annie," she said while swaying back and forth, making her dress rustle.

I didn't want to scare her, so I kept my hands in my lap. I desperately wanted to comfort her.

"Can I give you a hug?" I asked.

She nodded. I gently wrapped my arms around her and pulled her to my chest. Her little body snuggled close to mine. Her innocence and trust wrapped around me like a warm blanket. Her chubby fingers played with my long hair.

That simple act opened the floodgates of my grief. I sobbed for all the innocence we had lost, the fear and pain we had endured. By mentally separating, she had maintained our innocence.

"I'm sorry our childhood sucked," I said, wiping my running eyes and nose with the hem of my T-shirt. I held her shoulders away from my body and gazed at her adorable face.

"I know," she said. Her eyes held a timeless understanding.

"Everything is all right now. You're safe," I said.

Her big brown eyes stared back at me. "OK," she said quietly.

"I don't mean that bad things will never happen to us again, but hopefully it won't be like growing up with our dad." I hugged her to my chest again and whispered, "I love you so much."

She wrapped her arms tightly around my neck. I rocked her back and forth while I crooned "Twinkle, Twinkle, Little Star" under my breath.

Sometime later, I came to realize I was sitting on Dr. Chen's couch. My cheeks were stiff with dried tears, and my nose was stuffy. I wiped my face with my hands and reached for a tissue to blow my nose.

"How're you feeling?" Dr. Chen asked in her warm, soothing voice.

Taking stock, I replied, "I'm shaky, cold, and tired." My stiff muscles were slow to respond as I struggled to sit up. Gratefully, Grandma was in the lobby to drive me home.

"I'm not surprised. You've done some heavy emotional lifting." She handed me a little paper cup of water.

I took it and drank it down in one gulp.

"Were you able to communicate with your alters?" she said.

"Yes, I met two. A little girl around four and an adult woman."

"That's amazing," she said, leaning toward me. "It's incredible how you can set a purpose for yourself in these sessions and achieve them. It's truly remarkable."

Remarkable did not describe my bone-weary body. I sat up straighter and stretched my arms over my head.

Someone knocked lightly on the door. Dr. Chen glanced at her watch. "We've gone over our time. Are you OK to go now?" she asked, her brows furrowed in concern.

"Yes, I'm fine." I got up from the couch and headed to the door.

"When you get home, write down all the information about your alters that you can remember, and we'll discuss it next week," Dr. Chen said.

Dazed, I nodded and walked out the door. The now familiar hallway was blessedly empty. I kept my eyes and head down as I made my way to the lobby. I didn't want to be seen or acknowledge anyone else. I didn't have the energy.

CHAPTER 30

JESSIE

As Grandma and I approached our house, I spotted Rebecca on the road. I straightened in my seat and rolled down the window. "Hey," I called and waved as we pulled into the driveway.

Grandma parked, and I quickly jumped out of the car. Rebecca frowned as I jogged toward her.

"What's up?" I said as I squinted into the late-afternoon sun.

"Just wanted to see what you were up to. You didn't answer my text," she said.

"Oh, I had a therapy appointment, so Grandma had my phone in her purse," I said.

Her brow relaxed, and we automatically turned in the hot, humid air and walked toward Rebecca's house. Waves of heat shimmered in the air above the road.

"It's ridiculously hot," Rebecca said, wiping the sweat off her upper lip.

"Yeah, I'll be glad when it cools down. I hate the humidity," I said. I took the black elastic band from my wrist and pulled my heavy hair into a ponytail.

"How was it saying goodbye to Tim?" I asked. Since Rebecca and I talked and texted daily, I knew Tim had left for college yesterday.

"It was OK. We're keeping it pretty low key. I'm not allowed to officially date him anyway." Rebecca shrugged and appeared to take it in stride.

Her calm demeanor and acceptance impressed me. If Will had left for college, I would've been crying my eyes out. I quickly checked my phone, hoping he had texted me. No messages. My stomach sank.

"I'm pretty sure Brian told Tim not to date you as well," I said bumping my shoulder into hers. "Aren't you glad to be included under Brian's protection?" I asked.

Rebecca bumped back into me. "Oh yeah," she said with a laugh, "I may never have a boyfriend until your brother moves away."

"He *has* moved away, so here's your window," I said, smiling.

We walked through the slightly cooler dimness of Rebecca's garage and into her air-conditioned house. It was decorated in cool greens and light blue. The tasteful but comfortable furnishings made it a welcoming home. It was my safe space.

We headed back to her bedroom, our favorite hangout. I lay down on her thick, cream-colored shag rug, letting my sweat dry in the cool air.

Rebecca flopped down beside me. "What happened at Tim's party? Were you trying to piss Alex off?"

Ah, the real reason she came over to talk to me. I stared at the ceiling. I had been debating whether I should tell Rebecca about my dissociative identity disorder. I didn't want to burden her with it, and I didn't want to freak her out.

"Yeah, probably," I said.

Rebecca turned onto her side to face me. Her brow crinkled in a frown. "Why?"

I looked around her room. Did I want to risk losing my haven? This room, with its robin's-egg blue walls and awesome rug. And the most important part: my best friend.

"It's hard to explain, and I don't know if I should freak you out with some of the stuff I'm dealing with," I said.

"OK, now you have to tell me." She prodded my shoulder. Her brow was still wrinkled, her teeth biting her bottom lip.

I stared at her, trying to decide if I could take this risk. I exhaled and jumped off the proverbial cliff.

"If I'm angry or scared, it's like this other person takes over. My therapist thinks I have dissociative identity disorder, but most people know it by its old name, multiple personality disorder. It's a coping mechanism I created to deal with Dad."

Rebecca scrambled into a sitting position. "Holy shit!" she said, her eyes wide and staring. "How did you keep this secret?"

"I didn't want to scare you or make you want to stay away from your weird friend," I said.

Her eyes softened. "You're not weird, Jess. After all you've been through, I think you've handled it really well."

"Thanks." I lifted one corner of my mouth in an attempted smile. Counseling and discussions like this were taking a toll. Tears welled in my eyes in the face of her compassion. I had been gifted the best of friends.

"So how did your disorder cause the fight with Alex?" she said, furrowing her brows.

"When I see Alex, it hurts, and my anger at him comes flooding back. I guess Lena comes to protect me from the hurt," I said.

"Holy shit! Your personality has a separate name?" She stared at me, dumbfounded.

"Yeah, she does. Lena is a protector personality. She's older, stronger, and meaner apparently," I said. In my mind, I told Lena there was no need for her to come out. I could only hope that tactic would work.

Wow," Rebecca said. Her eyes unfocused and stared blankly into space for a moment. "A protector personality. This is so wild."

"She's not a threat to you or anything, but if I'm violent toward someone or very angry, just back away from me," I said.

Rebecca titled her head to the side. "How many personalities do you think you have?"

"I only know of two: Lena, my protector, and Annie, a four-year-old version of myself."

She nodded her head. "At least it makes sense now. The fight with Alex and the hot dog incident with Amanda. I mean, you're scary angry. It's a complete departure from who you are normally."

"I've heard," I said, grimacing. "I don't remember the things I do when one of my alters takes over. I only know what I've done because Brian and other people have told me."

"I'm glad you told me. I was starting to think you were developing a serious mean streak."

"For real!" I burst out laughing.

Do you mind if I check into it more?" Rebecca asked.

"No, of course not."

Typical Rebecca response. She would find out all there was to know about this disorder and how she could help me. We spent the rest of the afternoon talking about it. Tired and relieved, I walked back home for dinner. Rebecca would help me however she could, and I was grateful.

CHAPTER 31

JESSIE

The sun was inching toward sunset as I walked back up our driveway. The smell of barbecue wafting from the backyard made my mouth water. Barbecue chicken was one of my favorite dinners. I checked my phone again. My heart sank when I saw, yet again, that Will hadn't texted me. What if he wanted to break up with me after what Lena had done? The mere thought made me sick.

I started to dial his number and then remembered he was at work. *Call me when you get home*, I texted instead. Sighing, I put my phone back in my pocket and walked to the house dejectedly.

Baby waited for me at the front door, her little tail wagging vigorously. I smiled despite my sadness. I picked her up, snuggled her to my chest, and kissed her silky head. My little love always made me feel better. I followed my nose into the kitchen.

"Hi, sweetie. Are you hungry?" Mom turned away from the stove, smiling. She nibbled on a green bean pressed between her fingers. Her dirty blond hair was freshly cut and styled just above her shoulders, making her appear years younger. She was in a good mood. Did she block memories like me? She mentioned Dad less and less. Dr. Chen said it was a survival mechanism.

"Sure, what are we having?" I said just to be agreeable. My mouth was dry, and my stomach ached.

"Green beans, obviously," she said as she popped the rest of the vegetable into her mouth, "barbecue chicken and garlic bread."

"Sounds good," I said, smiling back at her. I stood there awkwardly for a moment. Functioning, normal Mom was a lot for me to process.

"Oh, do you want to watch some of *The Crown* with me after dinner?"

"Yeah," I said. I loved the show. British movies and books, like *Sense and Sensibility* and *Pride and Prejudice*, were some of my favorites. I loved the formality and precision in their speech.

The screen door slid open, and Grandma emerged from the back porch with a large plate laden with barbecued chicken. A gust of wind hastened her steps into the house. I peered out the patio door. The sky was suddenly dark with steel-gray clouds, and an increasing wind was pushing in from the south. The storm had come out of nowhere.

"Whew! There you are. I was afraid you would get caught in the storm," Grandma said as she laid the plate of chicken on the kitchen counter.

I filled my plate, then sat down at the dining room table. Brian's empty seat gaped at me like an open wound, and I did my best to ignore it. I would eat all my food in his honor. Smiling to myself, I snapped a pic of my plate and texted it to him with the caption *Thinking of you*.

"Eat your food." Grandma nudged my fork closer to my hand. I put my phone down and dug in. Barbecue sauce dripped onto my plate as I bit into the tender meat. The savory sauce was pure heaven. My phone dinged, but I didn't touch it with Grandma eyeing me.

"The chicken's great," I said. Ever aware of Mom feeling like second place, I took a big forkful of veggies and said, "The green beans are really good too." Not that I was a fan of green beans. They had a waxy texture. But salt and bits of bacon made them edible.

Tiny pebbles, twigs, and leaves pinged the windows as the storm continued. I turned toward the big bay window and noticed the dark-gray skies now had a tinge of pale green. It was late summer, long past the possible springtime tornados.

When I was six, Mom and I were watching Brian's Little League game when a similar rush of wind and storm clouds rolled in. That time, they'd been accompanied by the eerie, echoing sound of the tornado siren. Mom had gripped my hand and yelled for Brian. We rushed onto the field to get him, and he ran to meet us. Mom took his hand, and we all ran for the adjacent church basement. A man stood with door held open at the back of the church, hurriedly waving people inside.

The same pale-green tinge had painted the sky back then. It had excited me. The whole baseball team crowded into the basement. Mom put her arm around me protectively, and Brian scooted close to my side.

I had thought the whole thing was cool. Mom had protected us then. Now, so many years later, she was emotionally showing up again.

I finished up my dinner and took my plate to the sink. I rinsed it and put it in the dishwasher. Mom and I cleaned up the kitchen in a companionable silence. Thoughts of Will and why he hadn't gotten back to me ran around my brain. For the tenth time today, I checked my phone, but I only had a text from Brian: *I don't like you right now. The food sucks here.*

Smiling, I typed back, *Sorry bro.* I was sure he would figure out something he liked to eat.

The Crown's compelling, intense opening credit music played from the family room and got my immediate attention. I slid into the room just as it reached its soaring crescendo.

"Grandma, you started without me," I said, exasperated.

She smiled at me. "No, I figured hearing the intro would get you off your phone."

"Right," I mumbled and squinted at her. Mom patted the couch cushion next to her, and I plopped down. It was so weird to get Mom's attention. I wasn't comfortable with it. I didn't trust it would last.

The dark skies and stormy weather made it a good night to snuggle up and watch TV. Claire Foy, the actress who played Queen Elizabeth was compulsively watchable. I was completely taken in as the images flitted across the screen. It was good to lose myself in something I enjoyed. It was a much-needed mental break.

. . .

I walked down a long, majestic corridor with high ceilings and walls covered by large portraits. This was Buckingham Palace, I imagined. I gathered the sides of my silky, dark-blue ball gown, noting its halter neckline and open back, and carefully descended the grand staircase. A large, glittering group of royals and dignitaries awaited me below. As I approached, people greeted me with a curtsy and compliments. *I must be a princess or a queen.* I covered my mouth and giggled.

Searching the crowd, I found Will at last. My eyes were drawn to his beaming smile and intense stare. His blond hair was slicked back in the fashion of the fifties. With his athletic form and handsome face, he fit seamlessly into the elegant crowd. Like a magnet, I was pulled to him.

He bowed to me and then drew me into his arms to dance. The room changed into a vast ballroom with large windows lining the walls and ornate crystal chandeliers hanging from the ceiling. Will placed his warm hand on my exposed back and effortlessly twirled me around the room. A wide grin stretched across my face as I stared adoringly at him. I could dance in his arms forever. Nothing would please me more.

The ballroom darkened considerably as rain and wind pelted the windows. Lightning lit the sky and was followed by a deep, rolling thunder. The golden glow of the evening turned dark and heavy. The music stopped. I looked to Will for assurance, but I was no longer dancing with him.

The young version of my father stood in Will's place. He stared at me with soulless dark eyes and an ugly smirk. Horrified, I tried to pull my hands from his, but he squeezed them cruelly.

"Let go of me," I demanded, leaning backward and using my weight to try and pull my hands from his. I glanced around in a panic, but the ballroom had emptied as the storm raged. There was no one to help me. My tactic backfired badly as he used his weight to fall on top of me.

"You've taken my life. Now you're going to get what you deserve," he said. His dark eyes shined gleefully as his hands wrapped around my throat.

"You were going to kill me!" I spit in his face.

His weight pinned me to the floor. I struggled against him with no success. His hands tightened around my neck, cutting off any hope of air. I tried to use my strong legs to push his weight off my body, but he held still. I got my leg between his and kneed him in the groin. His grip on my neck loosened for a moment. Seizing the brief respite, I pushed myself out from under him, flipped over, and got to my feet. I had only gone a few steps when his fingernails viciously raked down my bare back.

Screaming, I came fully awake. I was on the floor of the family room with Mom kneeling beside me.

"Jess, honey. Jessie, it's just a dream." Mom pushed my damp hair from my forehead. I fought to come back to reality. The blanket from the couch was wrapped around my waist. We must have fallen asleep while watching the show. My back burned painfully. Groaning, I curled into a ball on my side.

"My back" were the only words I could utter.

Grandma rushed into the room. She was wearing pajamas, which meant she'd probably been asleep. My scream must have woken her.

"What's wrong?" she cried as she knelt by my head. An early morning light showed through the gaps in the curtains.

"He's trying to kill me," I whispered. Mom gently lifted my sweat-dampened T-shirt for a better look at my back.

"Oh my God! You're bleeding," Mom exclaimed. The cool air hit the wounds on my back, and I realized the scratches were real. Grandma scrambled next to Mom and gasped. My shirt was inched higher so they could view my injury in its entirety.

"Jessie! What happened? Who hurt you?" Grandma held her hand over her gaping mouth.

"Dad's trying to kill me in my dreams," I whispered.

"No, no, no. This can't be happening," Mom said seemingly to herself.

Emotionally, I was very far away. After several more attempts to get me to speak failed, Grandma gave up. She muttered "oh my God" under her breath.

She and Mom hustled me into the bathroom. In the mirror, I watched their horrified faces stare at my back and then at each other in bewilderment. They sat me down on the vanity bench. Mom's hand shook as she reached for a hand towel.

I chanced a glance at myself and quickly looked away. My hair was plastered to my sweaty scalp, my face had drained of all color, and my eyes were bleak and haunted. I was slipping from reality. Taking a deep breath, I began to internally repeat my name and address. It was the only tactic that kept my consciousness in my physical body.

Grandma applied antibiotic cream to the scratches while Mom scrounged through the bathroom drawers and cabinets for bandages big enough to cover them. She applied strips of gauze to cover each scratch and held the dressings in place with medical tape. Once done, Mom wrapped a blanket around my shoulders.

"Here, take these for the pain," Grandma said as she pressed two ibuprofen pills to my lips. She set a cup of hot cocoa on the counter in front of me. You could always count on Grandma to make something good.

I picked up the cocoa and swallowed the pills.

"Thank you," I muttered while keeping my eyes downcast. One glance at myself in the mirror would make me disconnect from this body.

"Why don't we go into the family room and watch TV," Grandma said as she prodded me to get up and walk with her. Mom followed behind. I sat in the middle of the couch, Grandma and Mom flanking me on each side. A happy, too-awake morning show host chirped the latest news.

"Jessie, can you tell me what happened?" Grandma gently asked.

I slowly turned my head toward her. "I did. Dad is trying to kill me in my dreams. He choked me and then scratched me when I tried to run away," I said numbly.

Grandma studied my face and then looked over my head to Mom.

I turned back to the TV and stared blankly at the screen until I couldn't keep my eyes open any longer.

CHAPTER 32

BRIAN

The insistent ring of my cell phone woke me up. Who in the hell was calling me this early?

I frantically fumbled around my covers, searching for my phone. Finally, I found it at the end of my bed. The screen glowed with the word *Mom*.

"Hello," I whispered, trying not to wake my roommate.

"I'm sorry to call you so early, but I need to talk to you," Mom said, sounding panicked.

Fear zipped through my body. Had Lena done something? I was suddenly wide awake. Nothing like a big jolt of drama to wake you up in the morning.

"What's wrong?" I whispered urgently. My roommate, Troy, hadn't stirred, but I needed to leave the room. "Wait. Hang on a sec."

I put down the phone and grabbed my crumpled jeans from the floor. I scrambled into them, followed by a T-shirt, and eased out of my dorm room.

"What happened?" I said. My bare feet made no sound on the nubby dark-blue carpet as I walked down the empty corridor toward the common room. The pale, silvery-blue light of early morning seeped in through the large, unadorned windows.

"Jessie woke up screaming this morning, and she has these long scratches down her back. She won't talk to Grandma or me, but she said she would speak to you," Mom said.

"What?" I exclaimed gripping the phone tighter.

"Just talk to her," Mom pleaded and handed the phone to Jessie.

I heard the familiar squeak of Jessie's bedroom door. "Hang on a minute," she said. Her door clicked shut.

"I had another nightmare with Dad, but this time he choked me and scratched my back for real," she whispered hurriedly into the phone, sniffs and hiccups littering her speech.

"Oh my God," I gasped. Her panic traveled through the phone. I sank into a chair in the common room. How could this happen? I believed her. There was no bullshit between Jessie and me. I rubbed my forehead. The psychic was right. I couldn't believe it. I didn't want to believe it.

"Were you wearing the pendant?" I asked.

"No," she moaned. "I forgot to put it back on after my shower yesterday."

"Go put it on and keep it on. You haven't had any encounters with Dad while you've had it on, right?"

I waited in silence. After taking a deep breath to calm down, I started to repeat my question, but she interrupted me. "Please talk to Mom," she begged. "She doesn't believe me."

"OK. OK, I will," I said, rocking nervously in my seat. I did have one idea. "Call Natalia, the psychic. Maybe she can help us."

"It's not working," she sobbed into the phone. "I haven't been able to hold the white light for any significant amount of time."

Jessie's door squeaked open in the background. "I have to know what's going on," Mom said, and she must have taken the phone because Jessie's sobs grew quieter and Mom's voice more distinct.

Resignation flooded my body. I was out of options and ideas. I scanned my surroundings. I was the only one in the room. The occasional whoosh and click from the air vents were the only sounds. No one would hear what I was saying.

I told Mom everything: Jessie's bad dreams and what a young version of Dad does in them. The presence we sensed walking around the house. And our conversation with Natalia.

"Why didn't you tell me any of this before? I could have helped you," Mom said.

Surprised, I sat back in the chair. She believed me. "I didn't want to upset you or cause you to worry. I mean, you spent months in a fog, barely noticing me and Jessie, and then you tried to kill yourself. You didn't need another stressor," I whispered urgently.

"I don't understand how this could be happening," Mom said.

"She's been talking about bad dreams for months," I muttered. Guilt clouded my thoughts. Should I have said something to Grandma or Mom? We really weren't used to taking our issues to adults. In the past, the adults had been the problem.

"Maybe I should talk to Reverend White about it," Mom said.

Ready to grasp at any solution, or at least give Mom something to focus on, I agreed. Jessie liked Reverend White. Maybe he could help. He had a calm and reasonable demeanor.

"OK, I will give him a call a little bit later," she said.

I clicked off the call and slumped forward, letting my head fall into my hands. I wanted to go home and see what was up with Jessie myself, but I didn't have a ride. Freshman weren't allowed to have cars on campus. The plan must be to trap us here until we got over being homesick. I wandered back to my room, quietly entered, and grabbed a sweatshirt, my wallet, and tennis shoes. Going back to bed wasn't an option.

In the quiet hallway, I shoved my bare feet into my sneakers. It was my first Sunday on campus. I'd been gone for one week and shit hit the fan. Typical.

The dining hall wasn't open yet, but I could walk to the coffee shop. Nervous energy made it necessary to move. Would any of my friends let me borrow a car to run home? I dialed Jessie's number, and it went straight to voice mail. It wasn't like her to not take my call.

Still holding my phone, I called Tracey. I had to tell her about this. She was my lifeline.

CHAPTER 33

JESSIE

I stood in front of Brian's dresser and pulled out his top drawer. Natalia's card was on top of assorted junk—unmatched socks, pens, pencils, and golf tees.

It rang three times before I heard her voice on the line.

"Hello, Natalia speaking," she said.

Hesitantly, I spoke. "Hi, Natalia. Um, it's Jessie Taylor. You met my brother and me several weeks ago. We came in about the ghost in our home."

"Of course, Jessie. How can I help you?"

The line was silent for a moment, and then I launched head-on into my story. "My Dad came into my dream last night, and he was trying to hurt me. And he did. He scratched my back in the dream, and when I woke up, I was bleeding. The gashes were real," I said.

"Were you wearing the pendant?" she asked urgently.

"No, I forgot to put it on after my shower yesterday," I said. It was such a stupid move. Guilt gnawed at me.

She sighed. "Please wear the pendant. It's protecting you."

"I have been. I won't forget again," I promised.

"Have you been practicing the white light?" she said. I could tell she already knew the answer.

"I can't hold the light. It fades out." My voice was a quiet rasp. I was hunched in the corner of Brian's dark room, praying Mom or Grandma wouldn't hear me talking on the phone.

"You did it naturally before in a dream. Focus on the people you love. Name them one by one. Think of why you love them; think of their love for you. Hold that love in your heart, and let it grow. Love is what maintains the light. Accept that, and it will come to you," she said.

She was so sure the white light would work. Her insistence pushed through the phone. I made up my mind. I would commit to practicing the white light every day.

"I will do it. I will create the white light around myself," I said with determination.

"Very good," she said.

Someone was coming down the hall. "I have to run. Thank you," I said and hung up. I quickly got up and returned the card to Brian's dresser.

Mom opened the door just seconds later. "How come you're in here?" she asked. "I thought I heard you talking."

"I was talking to Rebecca. But…" I waved my phone. *Oops, battery ran out.* "I'm looking for another phone charger. I thought maybe Brian left one in his junk drawer."

I shut his drawer, automatically hiding the business card. I didn't want to confide in her.

"Do you want to borrow mine?" she asked.

"No, that's OK. I'll just look around for mine. It has to be in my room somewhere," I said. I walked out of Brian's room and into mine. Mom stood hesitantly in the hallway as I slowly shut my door.

I lay down on my bed and turned on my side so my scraped-up back was comfortable. I was a strong person. Maybe if I thought of some examples of my strength, I would feel powerful enough to conjure the light and defeat Dad.

I had told on my dad for drinking. That was brave. I had tried to protect Brian when Dad hit him, even if I was hit in the process. I hadn't been afraid. I had asked Mom to kick Dad out of the house. That was brave too. Mom's doctor told me I'd survived. And survivors were strong. Confidence bloomed in my chest. Acknowledging these acts did give me a boost.

Now the white light. Closing my eyes, I placed both hands over my heart and took a deep breath in through my nose, held it for two seconds, and then slowly released it. By the third breath, my neck, back, and shoulders had relaxed. I imagined sparkling white light emanating from my heart. The black pedant was securely around my neck, and its comforting weight lay against my chest. It wouldn't be removed again until I was ready.

I thought of everyone I loved: Brian, Grandma, Baby, Rebecca, and Will. It was hard to include Mom on this list. Anger and sadness were tied up in my love for her. Instinctively, I knew thinking about her had weakened the light. The love had to be pure with no doubts. As I imagined each person, the light grew around my body and encompassed my entire room.

A wide, closed-lip smile stretched across my face, and a few happy tears trickled from the corners of my eyes. The light glowed and pulsed with energy. I could do this. Relief washed over me. The light held.

My phone vibrated next to me on the bed and broke my concentration. My hand slid across my comforter. I lifted the phone to my face and breathed a sigh of relief when the name Will glowed back at me.

"Hey," I answered, scooting myself into a sitting position.

"Hey." His subdued tone let me know all was not well between us. My stomach sank. We hadn't spoken since Tim's party. "Sorry I haven't gotten back to you sooner."

"That's OK," I said, gripping the phone to my ear. There were a few beats of silence, so I launched immediately into my apology. "I'm sorry about what I did at Tim's party. It was stupid, mean, and childish. I don't know what I was thinking."

He exhaled. "Yeah, it was pretty extra," he said. Sadness dripped from every word.

"I'm so sorry, Will. I know I hurt you and embarrassed you. And I never want to do that." The weight of what Lena had done was crushing. I had truly caused him pain.

"It just makes me think you aren't over him," he said.

His words were a blow. It was the worst possible scenario. "I am over him. I like you so much. You're ten times the guy he is. Please believe me," I pleaded. "Can we talk in person? Maybe go for a walk in the forest preserve?"

I prayed that if he saw my face, the emotion, the sincerity of how I much I loved him, he would forgive me. I couldn't bear the thought of losing his loving, happy presence in my life.

"Can you go in thirty minutes?" he asked.

"Yes." Relief flooded me. I would do anything to get us back to our usual easygoing happiness.

"See you in thirty," he said and clicked off.

I ran to the bathroom to triage my appearance. I washed my face with soap and water, then applied moisturizer, a little foundation, and some mascara.

Rushing back into my room, I stopped in front of my closet. *What should I wear?* I didn't want him to feel the bandages on my back, but I couldn't remove them. The scratches were still oozy and bloody. A sweatshirt was out of the question—it was too hot. I grabbed a tank top in a fabric thick enough to hide the bandages and a lighter, blousy shirt to put on over it.

"Mom," I said as I walked into the living room. "Can I go for a walk with Will in the forest preserve please? It would make me feel better." I shifted my weight from one foot to the other.

"I don't know, Jess. Is that a good idea?" she said, frowning.

"I'll be okay," I said, bouncing on my feet a bit. "Please? I already told him I could go."

"OK," she said, biting her lip, her brows furrowed with worry.

I was pretty sure my desperate face swayed her. Good thing because the low rumble of Will's jeep announced his arrival.

"Thanks, Mom," I said, rushing forward with a hug. Just as quickly, I turned, grabbed my bag, and headed to the front door. Will was already walking toward me as I emerged.

"Hey," I said. His lips were pressed together in a line. Relief washed over me just to see him. I suppressed the urge to hug him. I was worried, but I didn't want to broadcast it. He probably sensed it anyway.

He opened my car door for me, and I climbed in. We listened to "Sideways" by Citizen Cope as he drove to the forest preserve. I prayed Will heard the lyrics as I did: "These feelings won't go away / They've been knocking me sideways." He didn't hold my hand as he normally did. So, I reached for his hand and squeezed it. Thank God he didn't pull away.

We got along so well; we loved the same music, participated in the same sports. We were so right for each other. Fear creeped up my spine. What if he didn't forgive me? Did I need to tell him about Lena? Mentally, I shook myself. I couldn't do it; it was too weird. He might never talk to me again.

Will pulled into the forest preserve and we got out. The tall grass waved in the breeze. It was beautiful and peaceful here. Maybe the calm setting would help us bridge this gap. He didn't take my hand again, which let me know how much trouble I could expect. It wasn't going to be easy.

We silently walked along the path until we came to the bench we had sat on the last time we were here. He took a deep breath and began. "You know I really like you?"

"Yes," I said quietly.

"I asked you to be my girlfriend, which to me is a pretty big deal," he said.

"It is," I said. "And I want to be your girlfriend." I couldn't stand it anymore. I reached for his hand and held it in both of mine. My heart pounded.

"OK, but I don't want a girlfriend who acts like you did at Tim's party," he said and hung his head.

My heart plummeted. Was he breaking up with me? Every muscle in my body tensed.

"I don't want to act like I did at Tim's party either, and I promise I never will again." My eyes begged him to believe me. But could I keep that promise? I hated Lena for this. My gratitude to her disappeared.

"I don't know. The whole thing was really bad." Will rubbed his face and sighed. "It's happened before, like at Topher's party last year. I didn't mind then, but now I wonder if it's a pattern."

He was breaking up with me. The nicest boy I had ever met was pushing me away because of Lena. Cold fear and determination seized me.

"I have to tell you something, and it may make you not want to be my boyfriend. But I'll have to take that chance," I said. "I can't bear to have you think I'm someone I'm not."

Will studied my face with concern.

Taking a deep breath, I jumped into the proverbial icy water with both feet. "You know I'm going to counseling at the Oaks," I said and made eye contact with him.

"Yeah," he said, nodding.

"I need the counseling because my dad was abusive. He hit Brian and me, he tried to choke me, and he basically scared the shit out of me my whole life," I said.

Will's eyes widened in shock. "Jessie!" he exclaimed, moving toward me.

I held my palm up to ward him off. "Please, let me finish."

The worst was yet to come.

"His abuse caused my personality to fracture into different parts. If I'm threatened or very angry, a personality named Lena comes forward to deal with it." I sucked my lips inward and let him absorb the information.

His mouth dropped open and he just stared at me. "Oh my God," he said. Will and I continued to stare into each other's eyes.

"It doesn't happen all the time, but it does happen. A little girl named Annie shows up if I'm deeply scared."

Understanding dawned on his face. "The day of your dad's search, the day they found his body, you did act like a little girl. I thought maybe it was shock or something."

"It's called dissociative identity disorder. My counselor diagnosed me," I said.

Will rubbed his hand over his mouth. "I don't know what to say."

"Yeah, I get it," I said. He hadn't run away from me yet. I thought it was a good sign.

"I don't remember the things I do when Lena or Annie show up. It's a complete blank for me. Lena has it in for Alex, so she's the one who kicked him last year at Topher's party and a few days ago at Tim's party. I only know what I've done because Brian or other people have told me. My family, Rebecca, and you are the only people who know about my disorder." I exhaled forcefully. My secret was out.

"Is Lena going to come if you get mad at me?" he said, raising his brows.

It was a legit question. "I don't think so. She likes you. At Topher's party last year, it was her kissing you," I said, lifting one side of my mouth in a sad smile.

"Wow. Was it her kissing me in Tim's backyard?" He leaned toward me. I had his full, undivided attention.

Frowning, I said, "I don't remember kissing you in Tim's backyard, so it must have been her."

Will nodded his head. "You were a little more aggressive. Not that I minded," he said, hands raised to stop the apology teetering at the tip of my tongue. His smile said he didn't feel too weirded out. "But it was a noticeable change."

"I bet," I said. Sadness crept around my heart. Would he still want to be with me? "I hope with counseling I'll get better and learn to deal with my emotions without turning to Lena or Annie. But my doctor said it would take time."

Will continued to ask me questions, and we talked until the sun started to set. I didn't tell him about Dad's ghost or the scratches on my back. I was done sharing for the day.

We made way our way back to the Jeep and then to my house. We were both quiet. Who knew how he would take it. He cared for me, but would it be enough?

Before I got out of the car, I turned to Will. "Think about what you want to do. About whether you still want to be my boyfriend. I-I know I'm a lot to deal with," I said, desperately holding back my tears.

"Jessie," Will pleaded and extended his arms to embrace me.

I held up my hand. "I can't." I rushed from the car to the front door with my hand over my mouth to muffle my sobs.

CHAPTER 34

JESSIE

The next morning, Mom opened the front door for Reverend Wendell White and greeted him warmly. He had come by several times to sit with Mom when she was in her deep depression. He had prayed and read to her but hadn't pushed her to talk or interact more than she seemed able.

I loved how Reverend White would greet everyone with his version of a handshake, which was clasping your hand inside of his two large, soft ones. He was around five foot ten and had a slight belly and curly, light-brown hair streaked with gray. He was more like a professor or a teacher than a Reverend. He was one of the few men who I trusted instinctively. His kindness and peaceful demeanor eased the mood of most around him.

When I was confirmed into the Methodist church, Reverend White had led our group. He would laugh easily with us but take our questions seriously. As a thirteen-year-old, I'd really benefited from his kind guidance and direction; it'd had a positive impact on my self-esteem. Spending time in his calming presence was how I came to understand my father was far from normal.

Reverend White nodded at Grandma and said hello. Mom motioned for him to have a seat. He settled on our love seat and laid a brown leather briefcase by his feet. His kind and wise brown eyes found mine.

"Jessie how are you?" he asked. It wasn't a polite question. He meant for me to answer thoughtfully.

"I've been better," I said. He nodded his head.

"Should we discuss what happened to Jessie a few days ago?" Grandma asked. Mom had tearfully recounted the details of my nightmare and the scratches down my back to Reverend White this morning.

"If you don't mind, I thought Jessie and I could take a walk," he said.

Mom and Grandma looked at each other and then at me. "If it's OK with Jessie," Mom said.

"Yeah, that would be good," I said, surprised Mom had asked me. I rose from the couch and walked toward him. It would be easier to talk without an audience. I adjusted my shoulders a bit. The scratches had crusted over with scabs, and movement caused an uncomfortable tugging sensation.

Even while wearing the pendant, I was so keyed up at night, Sleep came in the wee hours of the morning, once exhaustion overwhelmed me. Mom or Grandma slept on an air mattress next to my bed. It eased my fear a little but not enough to let my guard down.

It had rained earlier and cooled what would normally be a hot August morning. The air was fresh, and the flowers swayed in the breeze.

"I talked with your mom, but I would like you to tell me what's going on," he said.

I repeated the condensed story: I believed my dad's spirit was haunting me, first attacking me in my dreams and now hurting me in the physical realm.

Reverend White nodded his head while he listened. "It's a lot to unpack," he said when I was finished.

A bark of a laugh erupted from my mouth. That was the understatement of the year.

I reached into the back pocket of my shorts and fished out my phone. My mom had taken a picture of my back, I guess for proof. I held it out to Reverend White, who furrowed his brows and stopped walking. He enlarged the image for a better view. Dad's nails had torn four long, angry scratches down my back.

"I know what your mom said, but I have to ask. Who caused these marks on your back?" His brown eyes stared into mine.

"It really happened in a dream. I think it's my dad," I said.

Reverend White took a deep breath and blew it out. "I've known you long enough to know you don't lie." He smiled gently.

I gave him a half smile in return. I had lied to people, but it was for my own survival. I didn't feel guilty about it at all.

"Why do you think it's your dad's spirit?" he said.

"In my nightmares, this swirling black orb sometimes morphs into a teenage boy. I didn't recognize him until I saw my dad's high school graduation photo a few weeks ago," I said. "Not long after that, Brian and I heard footsteps walking into the kitchen, but no one else in the house was awake. It sounded like Dad coming home from work."

Reverend White's brows drew together, and his face creased with worry. "Why do you think he would want to hurt you?"

"You know he had a drinking problem." Reverend White had been called several times by my mom to talk to Dad. Those talks affected Dad's behavior for a day or two, but that was all.

"Yes, I do," he said.

"It wasn't his only issue. He was mean. He hit Brian and me for the most ridiculous stuff. He was pretty rough with Mom as well." I was a million miles past caring what anyone thought of my father or my family. Surviving did that to you. It made you focus on what was truly important.

"Right before he died, I told Mom he had been out drinking the night before. She confronted him about it. I told on him, and he was furious with me. He went out drinking again that night and never came home," I said.

I couldn't explain my role in Dad's death any further.

Frowning, Reverend White began walking again, and I strolled at his side. He didn't talk or ask for more detail, which I appreciated.

"I'm sorry, Jessie. I had no inkling your dad was violent toward you. I thought he was getting the help he needed for the alcoholism."

"Yeah, that's the thing. No one wants to think your parents are mistreating you. It's too terrible. I get it," I said.

His shoulders drooped, and he turned to look at me. "I should have talked to you and Brian privately."

"We didn't tell anyone." I shrugged. "I wished we would have."

Sadness rolled off him, weighing heavy on me. I could have told him, but would it have made any difference? I sighed. The time for telling had passed.

"Please know you can always talk to me," he said.

We walked passed Rebecca's house. No one was outside. The neighborhood gossip chain would be activated if they noticed me taking a walk with Reverend White. He lived up the street from us, which might've given me a good cover story, but we didn't typically walk together. Emotionally, I was too tired to care. The neighborhood could discuss me to their hearts' content.

"Let's focus on what we can do now to help you," Reverend White said. "I would like you to pray for guidance and protection from harm. I would also like you to pray your father's soul moves on to his final resting place. Ask Jesus to guide your father toward peace." He gestured with emphasis while we walked.

My father didn't deserve any peace, but I would do it to save myself.

His conviction that prayer would help vibrated with every word. It reminded me of the certainty in Natalia's voice as she mentioned my guardian angels.

"Let's walk back and pray with your mom and grandmother," he said. I nodded, and we turned back toward the house. Our steps were quick with purpose.

When we got home, Mom and Grandma were perched on the couches in the living room in a tense silence.

"How was your walk?" Mom asked nervously. Her primary concern would be that I hadn't bad-mouthed her or indicated her failings as a mother. Grandma's pained face searched mine. I gave her a small smile so she wouldn't worry.

"It was good," I said, motioning for Reverend White to take a seat. I sat down next to Grandma on the couch.

"What do you think, Reverend White?" Mom asked.

"Well, I have had experiences with spirits before this, but not in a violent manner," he answered carefully while meeting Mom's gaze. "I'm sure you remember Mrs. Hoffman from across the street."

"Yes, of course," Mom said. Mrs. Hoffman had made us Christmas cookies every year, which made her near and dear to my heart. She had passed a few years ago.

"I was praying with her one day, and I clearly heard someone walking over the linoleum of her kitchen floor. Startled, I asked her if someone else was there," he said. "Mrs. Hoffman chuckled and said it was just Mr. Hoffman letting me know he was still around. And that wasn't the only time I heard his presence in her home. A few days before she passed, I was praying with her, and I heard his footsteps again."

I couldn't believe it. Was this a common ghost tactic? Make your presence known via creaking floors?

Mom smiled and nodded her head. "Yeah, I remember her talking about Mr. Hoffman making himself known after he passed. I hadn't really paid much attention, but I certainly get it now."

Reverend White rose from the couch. "Let's have a seat at the dining room table so we can join hands and pray," he said.

Grandma and Mom immediately rose, and I followed behind. We all took a seat around the dining room table. Reverend White held out his hands, and Mom and I each clasped one. I took Grandma's hand and so did my mom. Grandma squeezed my hand gently. We bowed our heads and Reverend White began.

"Heavenly Father, we thank you for being our protector. Please provide shelter to Jessie and her family from all hurt, harm, and danger," he said in a clear, strong voice.

"We humbly put our faith in your name, for we find our complete protection and safety in you, our heavenly father. May this home be a sacred dwelling for all who live within these walls. We decree that this home is now shielded from harm, illness, or misfortune. In God's name we pray. Amen."

Reverend White continued to bow his head. We all sat in silence, our hands clasped, until he was done. He sat up in his seat, released our hands, and blew out a breath.

The worry had eased from Mom's face, and Grandma was slightly more animated as well. Reverend White smiled at me reassuringly.

"How are you feeling, Jessie?" he said.

"I'm feeling OK," I said, trying to smile.

"OK." He looked at Mom and Grandma and said he would come back tomorrow evening to pray with us again.

I acknowledged his goodbye but remained at the dining room table, picking at the fringe on the place mat. In the back of my mind, I remembered Natalia's words: If this were a life lesson I was meant to overcome, neither my guardian angels nor God would prevent it from happening. My gut told me she was right. I was meant to endure and survive. I had to own my power to be free of him.

I ran through my mental list of times when I had been strong and brave. I would be free of my father

CHAPTER 35

JESSIE

Morning light filtered in through my bedroom window, peeking between gaps in the curtains. I stretched and then looked at the floor for Grandma. She had already vacated the air mattress beside my bed.

It was the first day of school. I sniffed and caught the aroma of coffee. Smiling, I pushed my covers down and shuffled to the kitchen. I entered to find Grandma on her hands and knees in the dining room, frantically picking up pictures from the floor. The china cabinet drawers stuck all the way out, and pictures were strewn across the table and the floor.

"What happened?" I said as I fell on the floor next to Grandma.

"Oh, Jessie. I didn't want you to see this," she cried. Her hands shook as she reached for more photos, and her face crumpled in distress. "When I woke up this morning, the drawers were hanging open, and pictures were flung everywhere."

I gathered two handfuls and dumped them into an open drawer. As I turned back to Grandma, I saw it. The high school photo of my father lay in the center of the place mat where I usually sat. Something shifted within me. My fear turned to rage.

I grabbed his picture and marched to the trash can. My fingers furiously tore it into pieces and let them fall into the garbage. Grandma, still kneeling on the floor, watched in silence.

How dare he continue to taunt me? For a moment, I wished he were here—physically here—so I could slap him across the face.

Grandma and I finished picking up all of the photos and returned them to their original jumbled mess. Our eyes met as I closed the drawers. We would keep this to ourselves. It wouldn't help Mom's mental state to know the love of her life was tormenting their daughter from beyond the grave. Sometimes I wanted to scream like a lunatic at the ridiculousness of it all.

"I guess the prayer didn't work," Grandma said as she poured me a cup of coffee.

I grimaced. "Well, at least I wasn't physically hurt."

"Yes, that's true." Grandma walked around the kitchen bar and gave me a hug. "If we need to, we will move out of this house and never come back."

I smiled at her. I liked the sound of that. This house had never felt like home. Unfortunately, I thought he would follow wherever I went.

I shoveled down my cereal and gulped the now warm coffee. It was time to shower and get ready or I would be late.

. . .

The whitewashed hallways of Valley Christian buzzed with excited greetings and whispered musings as students flooded its halls once again. So much had happened over the past six months; my view of myself and the world around me had grown exponentially. School had always been my safe space, but my usual enthusiasm to be back was tempered by the fact that my problems followed me everywhere now.

I smiled, nodded, and called out to other students as I looked for Alex. It was the first day of my sophomore year, and I had some apologizing to do. *Lena, don't even think about showing up.*

I could have called or texted him, but what I had done required a face-to-face apology. The alcove under the stairs, his usual hangout, was empty. I bit my bottom lip. How was I going to find him? I wanted to do this when I was ready, not when I randomly banged into him.

I turned to head to my locker and bumped directly into him. His hands came up to steady me. The subtle ginger smell of the cologne I had given him enveloped me. He still wore it. The scar on my heart throbbed a little. Alex had been my first love. He would probably always evoke some feeling within me.

"I'm sorry. I was looking at my phone," he said. Obviously, a lie. He bumped into me on purpose.

"It's OK. Hey, could we talk for a minute?" I said, looking up at him hopefully.

He motioned toward the alcove, and we both moved to the back wall for more privacy. His big, blue eyes, surrounded by thick, black eyelashes, stared down at me. I bit the inside of my cheek to help me focus. It had been a long time since I had stood face-to-face with him in this alcove. A lifetime ago.

Blunt was my mode of operation when nervous, and I stayed true to form. "I'm sorry for hurting you at Tim's party. I shouldn't have, and I wanted to apologize." I swallowed and stared down at my tennis shoes.

"It was pretty intense" he said, grimacing.

He shouldn't have charged toward me, but Lena had baited him. And what she did was inarguably worse. I took a deep breath. "Yeah, it wasn't cool."

He fiddled with the notebook in his hand. "So, you and Will are dating now?"

"Yeah," I said and then clamped my mouth shut.

"He's always liked you," he said bitterly.

I shook my head slightly, keeping my eyes on the floor. Will liking me was questionable. The pain in my heart flared with intensity. It had been two days since I'd revealed my issues to him, and I hadn't heard a peep.

"I'm sorry. I better go," I mumbled before walking away. He reached out for me, but I ignored his hand and quickly headed toward the girls' bathroom. I barely made it in time to stifle the sound of my sobs with my hands. Will not talking to me anymore was almost too much to bear.

I laid my hot head against the cool metal of the bathroom stall. Germs were the least of my worries.

CHAPTER 36

JESSIE

I took a deep breath and mentally pulled myself together. The constant drama was exhausting. Straightening my shoulders, I left the bathroom stall and washed my hands. I checked my makeup in the mirror and ran a finger under each eye to remove any smudged eyeliner. The girl looking back at me with sad, tired eyes was tan, and the sun had painted reddish-gold streaks in her rich, chocolate-brown hair.

I hurried out of the bathroom and up the stairs to my locker. A smile spread across my face as Kristi and Alli, my locker mates, came into view at our adjoining lockers. I quickly closed the gap between us and hugged them both from behind.

"Hello, ladies," I said as I squeezed between them.

Alli squealed, whipped toward me, and threw her arms around my shoulders. Kristi added to the melee. We crowded together and giggled in delight.

"Oh my God, it's so good to see you," Kristi said. We hooked our arms together and walked toward homeroom as one unit. If I was a topic of conversation in the hallways, I didn't notice. The joy of being with my friends again filled me up.

We reached our homeroom, and I rushed over to hug Holly, who was already seated. The four of us leaned out of our seats, heads bent toward one another as we quietly talked.

With so many of my days spent in counseling, I hadn't been around them much over the summer.

The bell for first period rang all too soon. I headed to my first class alone. As I walked the halls, several classmates greeted me, but there were a few who hung back and stared at me like I was a freak. The whole town was undoubtedly aware of my mom's mental state and my attack on her doctor. It was juicy gossip indeed.

Amanda, Alex's side piece from last year, walked past me but didn't make eye contact. After the beatdown Lena had given her, I didn't blame her for avoiding me like the plague. I had quite the reputation as a bad bitch, but my friends still stood beside me. Thank God.

Like the sun peeking out from behind the clouds, Will appeared at the end of the hallway. He smiled like he was happy to see me and walked toward me. A smile spread across my face as I quickened my step to greet him.

"Hey, I couldn't find you this morning," he said.

It was a relief to know he had been looking for me. Wanting no secrets between us, I rushed to fill him in on my talk with my ex. "I apologized to Alex this morning for how I acted at Tim's party. I thought it should be face-to-face based on what I did."

Or more accurately, what Lena had done.

Will frowned for a moment before he spoke. "Oh, how'd it go?"

"Fine. He accepted my apology," I said with a shrug.

"Nothing else? He didn't want to keep talking?" He studied my face intently, watching for my reaction. I was thrilled he cared. Maybe there was still hope for us.

I pressed my lips together for a moment. "He did, but I told him I had to go." Our eyes met, and Will just nodded.

"I'm sorry I haven't contacted you. I wanted to, but I was nervous as well. You're going through so much, and I had to be sure I could handle it," he said, his eyes imploring me to understand.

My heart threatened to pound out of my chest. *Please don't break up with me at school. I don't want to cry my eyes out here.*

"Are you going to break up with me?" I blurted. I couldn't take the suspense.

"No, I'm not," he said clearly as he pulled me into an embrace. "I couldn't stay away from you if I tried, and I don't want to try." His lips brushed the top of my head, muffling his words in my hair.

Relief flooded my body. I melted into him. I tilted my face to his for a kiss, and Will happily obliged.

"Get a room," Alli said as she sauntered by. Will and I separated, but I could only grin as Alli looked back at me.

Will put his arm over my shoulder and walked me to my class. All my worries slipped away for a bit.

CHAPTER 37

JESSIE

I walked the now familiar corridor to Dr. Chen's office. It was helpful to talk to my therapist, but I would've preferred to be out with Will and my friends. I knocked lightly on her partially open door.

"Yes, come in," she said from behind her desk.

"Hey, Dr. Chen," I said. She wore a long, yellow sundress with short sleeves.

"Hi, Jessie. It's good to see you. How are you?" she said.

"I'm fine." I picked up the rake in the little sand garden on the coffee table and started making designs.

"Hmm, you don't seem fine based on your lackluster response," she said, smiling.

Wow, she was going for it right out of the gate. "I mean, summer's over, and I've spent most of my time in some sort of group therapy or counseling. It's not how I wanted to spend my time," I said, not mentioning my dad the killer ghost.

She nodded in agreement. "I get it. But let's focus on how it's helped you."

"OK," I said, attempting a smile but landing on a grimace.

"What have you learned so far?" Dr. Chen asked.

I thought about it for a minute and then blurted the first thing that came to mind.

"That I don't like counseling," I said and burst out laughing. "I'm sorry. That was just too easy."

Dr. Chen chuckled along with me. Our eyes met, and she gazed back at me with amusement. "OK, what else?"

My brows creased as I gave it some real thought. "I learned why I have dissociative identity disorder and how it affects me," I said.

"Nice, I'm glad I've been of some help," she said. "Is there something you would like to discuss today?" Her brows rose questioningly.

Brian had urged me to control Lena, but I wasn't sure exactly how it worked. Would my request be enough?

"There is something. How do I control my alters? I don't want them to show up anytime there's trouble—or maybe ever," I said wrinkling my brow.

"Great question. I wanted to talk with you about it," she said, leaning toward me. "It wouldn't be about control. In clinical terms, we call it integration. To integrate your alters, you must decide how much of them you want to assimilate into yourself. And then you would need to take ownership of all the thoughts, feelings, memories, urges, and other traits associated with them."

I sat back in my seat. It was a lot to take in. I would need to integrate all the rage Lena possessed. I shuddered. It would burn me alive.

"That sounds like a ton of work," I said, raking sand again. Of course it wasn't simple or easy. Oh no. My life didn't function like that.

"It is work, but we can make it manageable. One step at a time. I know you can do it." She paused for a moment. "Think about how much of Lena and Annie you would like to integrate."

"I guess I assumed it would be all of them. Aren't they just parts of me, broken off to deal with my father?" I asked.

"Yes, very good," she said encouragingly.

"How can I integrate all the rage Lena has within her? I asked bewildered. "Won't it harm me?"

"You already have incorporated it to some degree. You recognize her rage; you understand what caused it, and you're working toward healing. You've done so much to heal yourself already. Give yourself some credit," Dr. Chen said.

She scooted off her chair and kneeled beside me. "One step at a time, Jessie. I promise I will help you all the way."

I lifted my head and our eyes met. She stared earnestly back at me. Taking a deep breath, I nodded my reply.

We talked for a little longer, and then I was back out in the hallway and headed to the parking lot. I was exhausted from it all. Mentally, I pushed aside the imagined emotional work piling up in front of me. Instead, I imagined one step at a time.

CHAPTER 38

JESSIE

I stood looking out my bedroom window at the gold and yellow leaves on our trees. Fall was my favorite season; I loved the cool, dry air. With my fuzz-prone hair, humidity was not my friend.

I held Baby in my arms and rubbed her silky ears before putting her down on the bed and fishing the black tourmaline pendant out from under my sweatshirt. The black hexagon shone in the palm of my hand. I had worn it without fail for the past few months, and it had done its job. Thank God.

Dad continued to cause trouble in the house. Lights burned out, doors slammed shut, and pockets of cold air appeared out of nowhere. But there were no physical attacks. Still, Baby hid under the dining room table during each incident, and Grandma was so freaked out she was determined to sell the house. She was working Mom hard on the idea of a fresh start in a new home. I would tell Grandma that Dad's ghost would follow me wherever we went.

With each scare tactic from Dad, my resolve to cast him out of our lives grew. I surrounded myself with white light every morning before I got out of bed. I set my intention for protection and only good things to come to me. When Dad was no longer an issue, I would continue this practice. My mood was better, more stable, because of it.

It was Halloween. The first trick-or-treaters were just ringing our doorbell. A pirate and a fairy ran through our front yard, their eyes glowing with excitement. I smiled at each of them. I loved kids, with their innocence and endless energy.

Tonight, after all the trick-or-treaters had gone home and Mom and Grandma had gone to bed, I would sneak out of the house. I would run to the foxhole with bare feet, just like last time. Dad would no doubt answer my call, and I would deal with him for the final time.

CHAPTER 39

BRIAN

The bass slamming out of the speakers vibrated through my body. The Halloween bonfire was rocking around me. What about fires, midnight, and Halloween brought the freak out in everyone?

My prisoner costume was lame, but with late notice, it was all I could find in my size. Tracey, however, was killing it in an adorable cat costume. The fitted black bodice and tights showed off her gorgeous body. I literally could stare at her all night long and never tire of it. She and my resident advisor, Kevin, were playing a game of quarters. Two tables had been set up about twelve feet apart, and competing teams were trying to land their quarters in the other team's cup. Tracey straightened her body and tossed her quarter. It arched upward, easily covering the distance, and dropped into the other team's cup.

Kevin and Tracey high-fived. Their smiling faces were flushed from beer, the fire, and fun. The opposing team, two guys I recognized from my dorm, guzzled the beer and removed the quarter. When it was their turn, the quarter sailed through the air and landed in the grass next to the table. Kevin hooted and hollered.

A slightly tipsy, giggling Tracey, twirled around and threw the quarter from over her shoulder. Again, it sailed through the air with a perfect arc and dropped neatly into the cup. Kevin and Tracey stared at each other with mouths hanging open.

"Oh my God! I can't believe that went in," Kevin yelled in Tracey's face.

"I know!" She yelled back.

One of the guys from the other team fell to his knees in the grass and covered his face.

Laughing, I couldn't wipe the smile from my face. I was having a blast just watching them. I was happy just to be in Tracey's presence. I had missed her so much.

A not-quite-full moon loomed overhead, adding to the general excitement of the bonfire. The party had been going for hours, and things were starting to get crazy. I stepped back as one of my goofball peers ran past me with a burning stick held over his head. And he wasn't the only one. It was a nightmare waiting to happen. I shook my head. Alcohol made a lot of dumb ideas seem smart.

My pocket vibrated. I reached in and pulled my phone out. Panic overcame me as I read the text from Jessie. My cup of beer dropped from my hand.

"No, no, no," I whispered. Gripping my phone, I dialed her number immediately. It just rang and rang. I ran toward Tracey.

"Hey, I'm sorry to interrupt, but I need Tracey," I said.

"Sure, no problem," Kevin said, his eyebrows shooting upward as he registered my panicked expression.

I pulled her aside. "We have to go to my house now. Jessie's calling Dad's ghost in the woods for some kind of showdown."

"Why? Why would she do that?" Responding to my urgency, Tracey turned and ran toward the parking lot.

"I'll tell you on the way," I said, jogging to her car. Thank God she was here. We desperately needed her car to get to Jessie in time.

CHAPTER 40

JESSIE

I texted Brian, set my phone to vibrate, and then laid it down in the grass. He would know where to find me if this all went to hell, but without a car, he would be too far away to intervene. I wouldn't take the chance he would be hurt.

My fingers confidently found the black string around my neck. I lifted the pendant necklace over my head. It slid from my hand to the ground.

It was the perfect night for this. The moon was almost full above me. It was missing the tiniest sliver. The fall breeze caressed my face and lifted my hair. And it was Halloween, the night when the veil between the living and the dead was the thinnest.

The foxhole we had built as kids loomed before me. The earthy smell of churned dirt, moss, and trees surrounded me. It made sense that Dad should meet me here for our final battle. I had picked the place and time carefully.

I could summon and encircle myself with protective white light at will. It had taken months of practice, tons of effort, and sheer determination, but now if I set my intention for the white light to stay in place around me, it would. I lifted my hands heavenward to open my heart and call on the power of God's love and protective white light.

A tingling sensation flowed throughout my body, bringing a sense of rejuvenation, strength, and unstoppable will.

The power was mine. I owned it. I controlled it. It was my right.

Two figures—Annie and Lena—lingered in the light closely behind me. I never thought I would see them outside my mind. Their part in tonight's battle was an unknown. Just one small detail that concerned me. Their love and support radiated toward me, but would we be stronger as one? Would their separation weaken me somehow?

I shook my head. My thoughts needed to be laser focused on feeding and building the white light. It had to be as solid as its own entity.

I planted my bare feet firmly on the grass and squared my shoulders. I took a deep breath and began.

"Louis David Taylor, my father, I demand your presence. I call you through the bonds of blood to face me." My strong, confident voice echoed through the woods. Within my white light, the woods glowed with orbs of blue, green, pink, and yellow, which rippled in and out of various forms. In my heightened mental state, another reality became visible.

I was just beginning to feel the importance of my own soul, my own needs, and my own boundaries. The demand to honor my boundaries and the accompanying rage burned through my veins.

The light highlighted the approach of a swirling black shape resembling the tall, thin frame of a teenage guy. Still an immature, hateful boy. It figured that even in death Dad couldn't manage adulthood. Why was I not surprised?

The black shape charged toward me, growling and snarling like a rabid dog. He reached the white light of my shield. Slowly, visibly straining, he pushed his way inside. The glimmering light enveloped him like a heavy, wet shroud. He fell to his knees under the weight.

My stomach clenched at his presence. His nasty energy was invading mine. *No!* How was he within my protection? My heart sank. I wasn't strong enough to keep him out. The light should have stopped him completely. A trickle of fear ran down my spine like a bead of sweat.

He moved toward me, his movements faster than before. My shield flickered. Panic zipped through my body, sharp like a raw, exposed nerve.

I stared into his soulless black eyes. A smile spread slowly across his evil face. He straightened and walked toward me. Frightened, I backed away from him.

"I'm impressed," he said as he motioned to the silvery glow around us. "It's not enough to keep me out, but you did make it slightly difficult." He brushed imaginary dust from his shoulders to demonstrate how little my protective shield mattered.

He quickly closed the gap between us and forcefully slapped my face. My head reeled to the left. Before I could right myself, he viciously pushed me to the ground.

"Now you're going to pay for what you've done to me," he hissed.

I landed hard on my butt and elbows. The impact thudded up my back and jostled my brain. My fingers dug into the dirt and mossy undergrowth as I struggled to move away from him. Lena strode toward me, a wide-eyed Annie following behind her. *No!* I screamed to Lena in my head. This was my fight. She could not help me here, though she wanted to desperately. That truth vibrated to my core.

I shook my head to clear the buzzing sound. Crouched on one knee, I placed my hands in the dirt for balance. In my peripheral vision, I caught sight of a heavy black boot headed directly for my face. At the last second, I jerked backward, and the boot missed my head.

Annie whimpered behind me. Shocked by the sound, my body twisted toward her. She huddled on the ground five feet from me, covering her head with her chubby little hands. Overwhelming sadness, guilt, and rage tore through me, one emotion after the other in a matter of seconds. I wept for Annie, for the childhood my dad had stolen from me and for the senseless tragedy he had caused. And I raged—at this beast of a boy with cold, dead eyes and at the man he once was. I titled my head back, opened my mouth, and screamed. Lena's screams joined with mine.

No! I would not be a victim again. It was so ridiculous, so out of bounds, I would not allow it. The white light intensified and crackled with energy. My father yelped and jerked with pain as the light stung him.

Panting, I finally made it to my feet. I turned again to see Annie. The ribbon around her red-checked dress trembled as she did. The sheer audacity of this man was dumbfounding.

Pure energy flared, pushing Dad away from me. *Yes, get away from me, you worthless shit.* His treatment of me had never been OK, not in the tiniest bit.

I picked up Annie and squeezed her to my chest. "He," I said as I pointed to our father, "will never touch us again." The conviction, the truth of what I said, was tangible.

Lena stepped toward me. "You're ready. You can handle him," she said with a knowing smile.

Chills erupted all over my body. We stared into each other's eyes; some final transfer was taking place. She closed the gap between us and merged into me in one fluid movement.

A sonic boom rippled through the white light. The force lifted and propelled my father completely out of it. Owning my own protection, my responsibility to honor myself, had pulled the pieces of my fractured mind together. And it wasn't done.

Annie gazed up at me with her big brown eyes and smiled.

"I love you," I said.

"I know," she said and hugged me tightly. Love, pure, strong, and unshakable, flowed through me. A golden glow emanated from my heart. Annie stretched upward and kissed my cheek.

"Thank you," she said.

Our eyes met and locked. She began to fade and then disappeared into my heart, as did the golden glow. The love was overwhelming. My legs gave out beneath me, and I crumpled to the ground, sobbing. It was finally over. It was hard to comprehend. Relief swirled around my body and brain like a healing cloud.

It didn't matter where Dad was or in what form. He had disappeared from my view, and I no longer sensed his presence. He could tool around this planet all he liked, but he would stay away from me.

The white light of my shield slowly faded. I no longer needed it. All the protection I required was within me.

CHAPTER 41

BRIAN

Tracey gripped my thigh as I raced over the hills and winding roads that led home. The dashboard clock glowed twelve thirty in the morning. Normally it would take forty-five minutes to drive home, but I was increasing my speed as much as I could without endangering my life or Tracey's.

To her credit, Tracey hadn't told me to slow down. She probably knew I wouldn't listen. Dad's ghost could have been choking the life out of my sister as I sped toward her

We had spent many nights on the phone talking about Dad's ghost and how he continued to terrorize Jessie. She listened and worried along with me. But to go up against him like this...

God, please help her, I begged. When would we ever be free of this bullshit? I hated Dad with a passion that had no bounds. I gripped and released the steering wheel repeatedly.

Tracey, rocking in her seat, stared straight ahead at the road.

Should I call Mom? I envisioned her standing there, helpless as Jessie died. I shook my head. Mom would not be able to help and seeing Jessie like that would destroy her mental stability for good.

As we neared Stanton, the hills subsided and gave way to flat land. I accelerated even more, flying across the dark landscape. I hoped there were no cops to pull me over.

By the time I made it to our street, the clock read a little after one. I skidded to a stop at the dead end that led to the woods. Leaving my lights on, I jerked my car door open and ran for the foxhole. The moon offered some illumination, but not enough. I clicked on my phone's flashlight and pointed it at the ground. Tracey followed a few yards behind me. The woods were silent around us. *God, please let her be OK* was my mind's constant refrain.

As I neared the foxhole, my light landed on Jessie's crumpled form. She wore a gray sweatshirt and jeans, and her bare feet were dirty. Though her face was turned away from me, I knew this was my sister.

"No!" I screamed as I dove beside her. This couldn't happen. Tears ran down my face.

"Oh no," Tracey cried. She knelt beside me, her hand on my back.

I gently turned Jessie's head. Her mouth hung open, and her eyes were closed. She was ghostly white, except for an angry red handprint on her swollen cheek. I put my ear to her chest. My eyes closed in relief at the sound of her thudding heart.

"She's OK," I said.

"Oh, thank goodness," Tracey said on an exhale. She scooted closer to Jessie and smoothed her hair away from her face.

"Jessie, can you hear me?" I said, hovering over her. "Jessie." I shook her shoulder slightly.

Her eyelids fluttered, and her hand rose to shade her eyes from my flashlight. I shifted the beam, and it caught on something in the grass by her head. The black pendant. I reached over and shoved it in my pocket.

"I'm OK," Jessie mumbled. "It's finally over." Her eyes met mine. The uncertainty I had so often seen in her gaze was gone.

"Let's get you home. Can you walk?" I said.

"Yes," she said, but she struggled to sit up. Tracey and I lifted her by her armpits, and she wrapped her arms around our shoulders. We stumbled out of the woods together. I desperately wanted to know what had happened, but it would have to wait.

I put Jessie in the back seat and made the short drive to our house. I breathed a sigh of relief when I noticed the lights were off. Tracey and I maneuvered Jessie onto the family room couch. I grabbed a blanket and covered her grass- and mud-stained clothes.

"Thank you," she mumbled and closed her eyes.

My gaze found Tracey. I walked over to her and wrapped my arms around her. It was over. The certainty of it coursed through my veins.

I leaned back so I could look into her eyes. "Thank you," I said, cradling her face in my hands. Her support meant everything to me.

She shook her head as tears welled in her eyes. We embraced again and stood there clinging to each other for a very long time.

CHAPTER 42

JESSIE

The months had flown by since my showdown with Dad. He hadn't returned, but I wouldn't be afraid if he did. A permanent shift had taken place within me. I had learned to stand up for myself. I would no longer be silent or complacent if someone hurt me or the people I loved. I would talk and tell every responsible adult I could find until someone listened. Counseling would be part of my life as I continued to heal, but I had crossed the biggest hurdle. Dr. Chen thought I had integrated my alters as well. She was amazed it had happened so organically. She didn't know my life had depended on it. The story of fighting Dad's ghost in the woods was just too weird to tell.

I no longer experienced missing time or those blinding headaches. All was right in my world. Mom was better, and we were working on building a functioning relationship. Giddy from my lack of worry, I smiled and giggled a lot.

I paced in front of our bay window, waiting for Brian to get home. Baby watched me from her perch on the couch. The winter sky was steely gray, but the ground was dry. A brisk wind made it seem colder.

It was the weekend, so Brian was taking me car shopping. I would have my license soon, and Mom was more than happy to provide me with a car so she could stop driving me to and from choir and track practice.

The low purr of Brian's muffler alerted me to his presence. Right after he pulled into the driveway, I grabbed my coat and purse and bounded out the front door.

"Hey," I called, waving as I strode toward his car.

Brian rolled down his window. "Can I not even step foot in the house?"

"No." I opened the passenger door, settled into my seat, and said in a lower voice, "I've been waiting for you all morning."

"Hang on," Brian said. He reached over and popped open the glove box. He grabbed a bulky white envelope and handed it to me. It gaped open.

My brows raised in question. "What's this?"

He didn't answer, so I shook the contents into my open palm. The black hexagonal pendant dropped into my hand. "Oh, I didn't know you had this," I said, warmth filling my chest. "I had thought about going back to the woods to see if I could find it."

"It was by your head in the grass when I found you that night. I thought we should give it back to Natalia and let her know we didn't need it anymore," Brian said, meeting my gaze.

"I love that!" I brought the pendant to my lips for a kiss. It had protected me well.

"I thought you would," he said.

I handed it back to him, and he dropped the pendant into the small envelope and then put it in a bigger envelope. Once it was addressed, stamped, and ready, Brian pulled up to our mailbox, and I rolled down my window to put it in. I could envision Natalia's pleased expression when she received it. That chapter of our lives had ended.

"Thank you," I said, smiling at Brian.

"No problem," he said, lifting one corner of his mouth. "All right, let's do this," he said while gripping the steering wheel. "Do you have some cars you want to see?"

"Uh, yeah. I have my list in my phone," I said, waving it at him.

"OK, where are we going?"

"Not far, actually. Just a few streets over. This guy is selling his used Nissan 370Z," I said, raising my brows hopefully.

Brian paused at the stop sign and stared at me. "Are all the cars on your list unsuitable? 'Cause we're going to my list for better options."

"What's wrong with my pick?" I said indignantly. I had already imagined myself zipping around town in the sleek, black, sporty two door.

"It's too small. If you got in an accident, you would be squashed like a bug," he said, shaking his head. "Next pick."

The neat ranch houses rolled by as we drove. Our arguments were mundane and oh so normal now. That realization snuck up on me at times and still surprised me.

As I stared out the window, I caught my smiling reflection looking back at me. I wasn't afraid of meeting my own eyes anymore. The haunted look no longer remained.

Whatever happened, good or bad, I would be OK.

• • •

THE END

ABOUT THE AUTHOR

LeeAnn Werner is an author, speaker and marketing consultant. LeeAnn holds a bachelor's degree from Bowling Green State University in Journalism. She lives in Illinois with her wonderful husband, three beautiful children and two rowdy dogs. You can check out her web page and blog at www.illusionofagirl.com.

Amy Goray Photography

Made in the USA
Las Vegas, NV
28 October 2021